G000136211

For Matt and his flying club,
there weren't any options left.
Trapped residents, threatened towns
and one small airstrip safely upwind of the fire.

It's not a promising position, but they volunteer,
hoping one plane might make a difference.

And then the wind changes.

The first novel by VH Folland

Fire Season

VH Folland

FIRE SEASON

First published in Great Britain by Ragged Angel Ltd

ISBN-10: 0-9541227-7-1
ISBN-13: 978-0-541227-7-5

The right of VH Folland to be identified as the author of
this work has been asserted in accordance with the
Copyright, Designs and Patents Act 1988

Cover painting by Barry Weekley copyright © 2010
Copyright © VH Folland 2010
Publisher: Ragged Angel Ltd, 409-411 Croydon Road,
Beckenham, Kent, BR3 3PP.

To Fred, with thanks for a
lifelong love of aviation

The Day Before

When the wind changed it brought the smell of smoke to the small town. The season's fires were still a few hundred miles away, but the conflagration as the peat forest burned was sending up a plume of smoke and ash that had carried far and wide.

Wiping off the front of his crop sprayer, Matt scowled in the fire's general direction.

"A bit of dust won't hurt it." Jake laughed, and Matt redoubled his efforts.

"Never an excuse for one of my aircraft not to look her best." He grunted, casting another dark glance skyward.

"He'll be fine. Stop worrying," Jake said as he watched Matt rub furiously at a spot with his chamois leather. Matt ignored him. Finally, Jake had had enough. He walked across abruptly and climbed into the cockpit.

"Hey, Whaddya think –" Matt stopped as Jake flipped the radio on, changing the channel to local aviation, and giving the older pilot a broad grin.

"There you go. If Rob's gonna crash you can hear it live."

"Bastard." There was no real sting in Matt's voice and, as Jake climbed out, the crop sprayer pilot made no move to turn the radio off.

"Look, he'll cram as many inside that little Robin of yours as he can, realise he doesn't know the first thing about airport flying and flounder her back here. You'll have houseguests."

"I don't want guests." Matt grumped, busily polishing Jake's imaginary fingerprints off the aeroplane's door.

"Tough luck. They'll be safe here and you know it." Jake bit out a little harshly, and Matt scowled. "Sorry. Last year it would've been me out there fighting the fires."

"They've got that bad now?" Matt paused in his cleaning as he asked. Not much could distract the old crop sprayer pilot, and the pause was more eloquent than a shout.

"Yes. They're calling the reserves in. Joy of a peat fire – you put it out one place, and it springs up in another."

"Nothing you can do to help," Matt said with grudging sympathy.

"Except take your unwanted guests." Jake laughed, and got a dry chuckle out of Matt.

When the scale of the fires had become apparent Matt, half-joking, had offered to loan the airstrip's touring plane, a small Robin four-seater, to the emergency efforts. To his great surprise his offer was accepted, an early indication of how bad the situation had become. His nephew Rob had left two days ago, initially assigned to the fire-spotting duties he had been trained for. Instead, from hurried phone calls between flights, Matt had learned he was flying the small plane hither and yon to the isolated homesteads where it could manage a field take off, to evacuate families and the injured to the airports designated as hubs for the rescue effort. Under the circumstances it was too easy to forget Rob's many years of experience crop spraying, surveying, and general aviation, and remember a gawky teenager getting his first lesson. Matt's concern, poorly hidden when Rob had left, was growing.

In this heat, with red ash in the air, he knew that the wood and canvas Robin was at more risk than most. Even if the aeroplane was flying miles from the fire, he had to fight down his concern for his aircraft – and his nephew.

"I'm heading for town to check the others are alright. You OK up here?" Jake asked, abruptly fidgeting. Torn between the desire to do anything to help, and dreading a call up to the front line, the former fire-fighter had been almost as on edge as Matt this morning.

"I'm fine. Been fine a long time before you came along. Get on with you."

Jake dodged the cleaning cloth Matt flicked at him, and walked back to his car. As the valley's fire marshall, he had his own duties to attend to, not least of which was making sure the fire could not start a new front here.

Matt waited until the car was long gone, the sound of the engine scarcely audible in the quiet afternoon, before he stood back and looked the plane over. He had to admit to himself that there really was not any more he could do to clean her. Instead, with the Robin gone, he walked into the hangar and turned his attention to the third and final aircraft in his collection.

A private sin, as he regarded it, the gunmetal grey shape dwarfed the two light aircraft that usually shared her hangar. On a dare, Matt had once tried to fit the Robin under one wing and very nearly succeeded. He blamed the resting position of the huge propellers for his failure.

It was ugly, immense, unflyable, and utterly useless. Matt loved it anyway. He had bought the damaged airframe from pure sentiment at auction and the Avro Shackleton, then more rust than metal, had been moved up here on a huge trailer truck. Even if she could fly, there was not a runway up here long enough for her take-off run.

All of which he knew. It did not stop him tinkering whenever he needed the distraction. Taking a rag, he carefully wiped oil seepage from one of the engines and smiled. The first time he had got one of the Griffon engines running, half the valley had been up here to find out what was going on. Now he was up to three at a time, and for the sake of neighbourhood harmony he had agreed to warn them before he ran any more engine tests. If he had more space she would be a ground running tourist attraction, despite the noise complaints, but as it was he had still turned the battered hulk into a good-looking aircraft.

After careful application of the welding torch and wire wool, the few patches of corrosion that remained were in cosmetic areas, but they all needed to be finished if he wanted her to look pristine. After all rust was the same process as fire, if slower, and just as destructive if allowed to run unchecked.

Matt stepped back in disgust. His distraction was not working, and everything kept turning his thoughts back to the fires outside the Vale. The nearest large blaze was over a hundred miles away, but it was disconcerting to smell smoke on the breeze instead of sea salt. Springing up early in the season, the flames had begun the peat smouldering underground before they were detected. The spell of hot weather had not broken throughout the summer and now, in August, the flames had tinder dry-foliage to feed on. The fires were rapidly growing out of control.

From the direction of the little fridge in the corner there was a brief flicker. Turning, he saw that the red light had gone out and the quiet hum was absent. He sighed and walked across, but although he waited a few minutes the power showed no signs of coming back on. The fire must have taken the power lines out again.

Matt threw a glance at the diesel generator and then dismissed the idea. The wind turbine on the side of the hangar would keep the reserve batteries charged for radio and lights. Otherwise, it was a lovely summer's day, he had a gas camping stove for cooking and if it came down to it the fridge would keep beer cool for a couple of hours. Thinking of beer he pulled one out of the fridge and opened it, taking a swig and wondering what to do next when the sound of an engine interrupted him. He walked out of the hangar to take a look.

The small airstrip was the closest building to the entrance to the valley, as far from the other houses as he could site it. People in general were happier that way, as the noise of the aircraft began early during the spraying season and few of the residents liked being woken. It also meant that he had a good view of the road over the hill that lead into the valley and early warning of people coming or going. Matt himself was happier that way. Now, there was a large four-wheel-drive truck coming up the road, its back loaded with supplies. As it turned up the road to the airfield, Matt frowned as he recognised his visitor, then went inside and grabbed two empty crates from the hangar. The large truck pulled up at the front, and the driver got out, pulling a couple of bags out of the passenger's side.

"Hi Matt. Your tins, cans and food supplies. Sure this is enough?"

"Yeah, plenty, Nick. Thanks." Looking quickly through the bags Matt nodded to himself before he dropped the shopping into the crates and shoved them into the hangar.

"No problem. What are neighbours for?" The retired trucker leaned back against the side of his car and Matt settled himself back on the crate, grateful for someone to talk to.

"Been busy?"

"House full of evacuees." The big man shrugged. "They'll be gone tomorrow, but meanwhile I'm on supply runs. I'm surprised you haven't got any visitors."

"Too difficult to keep them off the planes," Matt said, gesturing with his beer. Nick nodded sympathetically.

"I've the same problem with kids and the trail bike," he admitted a touch ruefully. "Their parents are afraid their house will burn down and they'll lose everything and all the kids want to do is carve doughnut trails in my lawn! Hey, aren't you down a plane?"

"Rob's taken it to help with the evacuation. He's been out a day or so now." Pride and concern both showed in Matt's careful tone, and Nick nodded in respect.

"Doing his bit. All we can do really – well that and wait for it to pass." There was a moment of silence as the two considered the situation. No one was really worried about the fires reaching the town itself. In its hundred and twenty year history Brooke's Vale had never burned. Sheltered in a valley, the bedrock close to the surface, the prevailing wind blew in from the coast to the north. Threatening fires were always blown south, away from the Vale. As a result the inhabitants of the valley had become used to taking in the strays and refugees from the summer fires until they had somewhere else to go, or were allowed to return home. This

15

year's fires had already brought a steady stream of evacuees through the valley, and the residents had done their best to offer a safe haven.

"Have you seen Rose around? The wife called and the radio's on the blink." Nick stretched his legs out, easing them from the cramped journey.

"Up at the Barnehursts, fixing the fuse box. She took Jim with her." Matt paused. With the power out again, the fuses had probably broken again as she fixed it.

"Jim doesn't know a thing about fuses!" Nick exclaimed in surprise and then grinned. "Private time with the boyfriend?"

"No, Jim's up there as designated man," Matt replied sourly. Nick rolled his eyes in agreement. Both Matt and Nick had had to drop tasks and head across to deal with Roger Barnehurst's attitude before.

"Lucky guy. Rather him than me."

"What I said." Matt took another drink. "Want a beer?"

"Ah, no. Sorry. In these conditions, you're never sure when there'll be more driving to do. I'm surprised you're drinking and not taking the crop sprayer up to give them a hand?" There was honest curiosity, not condemnation, in the question.

"Flying? In these conditions? There are experienced firefighters for that kind of thing. I'd just be in the way." Nick's eyebrows lifted at Matt's comment, and he leaned forward.

"That's the odd thing. I haven't seen any of the aerial firefighters, but there are a lot of cropsprayers flying about. Apparently there's a shortage or something. They're recruiting extra help."

"Yeah well, with Rob already out, someone's got to look after the airfield." Matt's face betrayed nothing, but his shrewd mind was beginning to work. He was never good at sitting still. Nick nodded in understanding and stood up, brushing himself off.

"Anyway, I'd better get the supplies back. See you later."

"Power's out again," Matt said, as Nick got ready to leave. "Looks like it might be out for a while."

"Thanks for the heads up. I'll fill up on diesel in town, just in case." Nick climbed back into the car, pulling away rapidly. Quietly in the background the radio reported the fire, now sixty miles from Lydford and moving east.

Matt tapped his fingers idly on the beer can as he thought about the fires. Sixty miles from Lydford seemed uncomfortably close, particularly for a pilot used to flying that distance in minutes. Turning the matter over in his mind, he decided he was less concerned that the fire front would enter Brooke's Vale and more that an incident within the valley would start a fire here. If that happened, Jake and his water tender would be the only way to control it until help could arrive. The fire marshall was only one person, despite his years of experience. A little extra help might be needed, and after all, the cropsprayer was right here.

With the ease of practice, he connected a hose to the tap on the side of the hangar, running the other end into the crop-sprayer's onboard water intake. No sense using up his own water reserves while they still had mains water pressure, even if it would be slower than the pressurised pump and groundwater well he usually used. Despite the remnants of chemicals and pesticides in the tank from previous spraying, a full tank still gave him an option if a fire should threaten the valley. Two thousand litres of water should slow a blaze down, at the very least. If he had thought about doing this earlier he wouldn't have been drinking, but consoled himself that the fire risk was low. After all, if it had not happened so far, it was unlikely to happen soon. Plenty of time to sober up, and in the meantime he could at least get the plane ready. Reluctantly he switched the radio off to save the battery.

Unfortunately, with water and fuel connected, that just left him to sit in silence. Another hour of uncomfortable shifting, small chores and impatient waiting passed before the sound of footsteps broke the silence. Grateful for a distraction, Matt walked round to the front of the airstrip.

"Jill!" he said, surprised and pleased although he would never show it.

"Am I welcome? The house was getting very quiet, so I thought I'd see how you were." His neighbour, accountant, and office manager, if indeed a two-pilot airstrip could be said to have one, smiled. Matt sat back down on his box and gestured for her to take a seat.

"What about your evacuees?" he asked.

"Moved on this morning. They've got relatives further out and they'd rather stay with family."

"Makes sense." Matt nodded, quietly revising his plans. If Jill was available to help that gave him an extra pair of eyes to look after the airfield.

"Actually, I'm glad to see them go," she confessed, running a hand through grey hair. "I thought I was done with a house full of kids when mine grew up and moved out. It gets more tiring every year."

"S'why I let my sister do the kid thing. Me, I've my planes." Matt gestured and chuckled, throwing a quick glance at the Robin's empty spot. Jill grimaced sympathetically.

"I heard about Rob. Must be tricky, letting someone else take your plane up when there's nothing you can do."

"Yeah, well. He had more hours in the Robin than I do. The crop sprayer only takes two and the Shackleton's a museum piece." Matt felt oddly defensive, and fidgeted slightly as he broached the idea. "I could take the crop sprayer up, I guess."

"But you don't know what you're doing, you'd get in the way of the actual fire-fighting efforts, and it would cost the earth in fuel." Jill nodded in sympathy as she voiced the issues they discussed every year. They had worked together on the airstrip so long that she had a good idea of the requirements of running aircraft, and the costs involved. "What brought this on?"

"Just a thought. Something Nick said." Matt shrugged. It had probably been an unlikely idea anyway, although the possibility of actually doing something instead of waiting here for Rob still tempted him.

"Seriously, Matt, no sense bankrupting yourself to try and help now. Wait until afterwards and donate the cash directly to the relief funds. There are going to be a lot of people needing homes." For a moment there was silence as they considered the recent events. Although it was a depressing topic it seemed inevitable that the fires were the only thing on anyone's mind at the moment. "And since you know this, may I ask why you're filling the sprayer?"

"Just thought, if anything started up in the valley, she carries a bit more than Jake's little tender."

"Good idea." Jill nodded, looking round for something else to discuss that would not inevitably lead back to the fires.

"Do you think I should help more in the valley?" Matt asked abruptly, drumming his fingers on the edge of the box in frustration.

"How? We're not having evacuees up here, not with the planes and not after last time. We've been through the flying issue."

"I could have gone with Jake on his rounds, or up to the Barnehursts with Rose."

"You'd volunteer to visit Roger?" Jill's voice was dry and amused.

"Well…" Matt looked at his feet.

"Thought not. Besides, they're heading back now. Looks like your flying club members are meeting up here." She nodded to the road where a small battered car was making its way up towards the airfield. Matt shook his head at her. It was perhaps inevitable that the airstrip, designed for use by the crop sprayer, had become home from home for the other pilots in the valley. There were only four however, so the "flying club" usually spent evenings talking aircraft and eating sandwiches, and not doing very much actual flying.

Parking by the hangar, the two new arrivals climbed out, wearing identical expressions of distaste.

"Hi, Rose, hi, Jim. Nice to see you." Jill put on her brightest smile and was rewarded with glares. "So how are Roger and Mrs Roger?"

"Loud, obnoxious and annoying. The other one is quiet, meek and invisible," Rose said disgusted, before heading into the hangar. Jill looked at Jim as his girlfriend disappeared to wash the traces of the Barnehursts off.

"That good?" she asked, and the younger man slumped down on a box.

"I just spent the morning repeating everything Rose said, understanding none of it, while Roger smirked at Rose and said he was just making sure. Next time his power goes, he can go without. What a waste of time."

"Well, at least his evacuees have power," Jill reproved and Jim laughed harshly.

"What evacuees?"

"But he told me – oh, that man!" Jill broke off, incredulous and fuming.

"Yep, he lied." Jim was plainly not impressed.

"Power went out again about an hour ago," Matt said, with a nod towards the fridge.

"Oh, what a shame. That would have been right as we left," Rose said without much sympathy, as she walked across towelling her hands dry. "Well, I'm not going back up there for him. No evacuees, no power."

"That's a point, where's Jake?" Jim asked suddenly.

"In town, why?" Jill answered, slightly thrown.

"I need to tell him he just spent the morning at the Barnehursts." Rose and Jim grinned as the others burst out laughing.

"Jake and Jim, the terrible twins? I take it Roger is better behaved with the fire marshal breathing down his neck."

"A bit," Jim admitted. "It's a useful trick. Almost makes it worth having a brother."

"Behave, you. I used to baby-sit you two and I have plenty of stories…"

"Alright, you win." Jim held up his hands in mock surrender at Jill's threat. Rose was grinning.

"Please?" she asked the older woman hopefully.

"Why waste good blackmail material?" Jill replied, and then relented. "Maybe I'll tell you later."

"Matt, mind if I have a look at the Shack?" Jim asked, trying to get away from a potentially embarrassing conversation.

"Feel free. I'll listen to the ladies." A wave of the beer and Matt grinned at Jim's sour face. The distraction was more than welcome, but the sound of a familiar engine brought him back to the matter at hand. As the car drove up, he wandered across for a better look.

"That's Jake," Jill said, peering at the road. "Thought he was in town?"

"Must want something." Matt shrugged laconically. They waited as the car pulled up, towing the fire marshall's small mobile water tender behind it. "Jake?"

"Hope you don't mind if I use your well and pump? I need to fill the tank, and mine's just broken."

"Typical." Jill rolled her eyes and gestured across. "Too posh to use a hosepipe and tap?"

"No, just don't have the patience," Jake replied, driving up to the ground-water connection. He gave the crop sprayer a wide berth. If any of the hoses damaged it, he would be hearing about it from Matt and Jill for months, and probably paying for the repairs. He took a breath, staring at the unfamiliar setup, and began to fiddle with the connections until Matt went across to give him a hand.

"Hey, Colin's coming back." Jim was looking over the rise at the road in, leaving his brother to struggle with the tender.

"He headed out for supplies earlier. He might have some news," Jill said, as the truck turned up towards the airfield. It pulled in a few minutes later, and the athlete jumped out.

"Hey," he greeted them, looking round at the group.

"Hay is for horses," Matt grumped back, but grinned as Colin held up a can with a winning smile.

"The extra oil you needed?"

Matt took it off him and looked it over before he nodded.

"Perfect. Whadda I owe ya?"

"Call it even for those diesel cans you offered. Just getting some supplies for the generator. Power's out again, if you didn't already know," Colin explained. He took a look at the pair working on the water tender, but obviously decided that shorts and a polo shirt were not the best things to wear when tackling a filthy water pump and left them to it. "I just got back from Lydford."

"So, how are they doing out there?" Jill asked the question on most of their minds.

"Not great. There are hazard warnings and a lot of people choosing to get out now rather than wait for a signal. The firemen aren't having a lot of luck putting it out."

"It's a pine forest with peat layers after a long hot summer. Whatever started it, it's not going to be easy to put out," Jake said, as they heard the sound of water beginning to flow into the tender. Satisfied with his work he straightened up, leaving it to fill.

"Do they know what started it yet?" Rose asked, and Jake shook his head.

"Started which one? It's hot, dry and there's been more than a few. The last set sprung up when the power lines came down around Lydford, but before that who knows? They've been run ragged all summer trying to keep things under control." He shifted, uncomfortably aware that until last year he would have been out there with the fire crews. "I'll head round, soak down the worst of the danger zones, try to make sure anyone in Brooke's Vale who's at medical risk is out, the usual. There's not much more we can do."

"You know, I don't know why we're doing this," Rose said, thoughtfully "This is somewhere people run to, not from. Half the houses have refugees in them. Brooke's Vale never burns."

"Just as well," Jake said quietly.

"Sorry?"

"If fire ever came here, it would be nasty."

"I'll take your word on it." Rose looked doubtful, and Jake rubbed a hand against his head, wondering how to phrase an answer.

"Think about it. There's one way out of this valley, unless you can fly. The cliffs are too steep for most vehicles. If fire blocks that road, then you're trapped. When it comes into the valley, the cliffs and hills will channel it, funnelling the flames into a firestorm."

"But with all the damp vegetation it would never catch hold," Colin said, and Jake shook his head.

"Most of the trees are pine. In this heat they emit sap to help keep them hydrated, but the sap is highly flammable. Think of them as telegraph poles soaked in naphtha. Some of the decorative plants are as bad, since the gases they emit in heat are flammable themselves. Look at the Stilsons' rosemary border – that's notorious for causing fires. And with the shape of the valley and the wind blowing from the other direction these gases aren't being removed as they normally would." Jake stopped, suddenly aware that he had fallen into fire safety mode, and was being viewed with something akin to horror by his audience.

"Thanks. Suddenly my nice, safe, home doesn't feel very safe anymore." Rose filled the silence with everyone's thoughts.

"Well, it hasn't happened for one hundred and twenty years," Jake said lamely, trying to take the sting out of his words. He checked the water gauge on the tender but it was only half full, offering no easy escape from the conversation. Matt stepped in.

"Oy! Give me a hand with the diesel cans," he snapped, and Jake leapt at the excuse. Between the two of them, they manhandled the two heavy diesel cans out to Colin's car. By the time they had finished securing them the tender was full, to Jake's great and obvious relief.

"I'd better be off on the rounds shortly. Any chance you'll be leaving?" Jake asked hopefully, and Colin chuckled.

"We've had this chat already. We've got the pond, and water reserves, so we're as safe here as anywhere. Hey, the refugees are coming to us in droves," he pointed out.

29

"Eating you out of house and home?" Rose teased, and Colin guffawed before he turned back to Jake.

"Look Jake, I know you're just doing your job and I appreciate it, but do you really think Brooke's Vale is going up?" There was an awkward pause. Colin was not the only one waiting for the answer.

"No," Jake admitted truthfully. "But I have to plan for the worst."

"Good. Then there's nothing to worry about is there? I'd better get this back to the house." Colin gestured at the diesel cans, and climbed into his car.

"Nice guy," Rose said as they watched him leave.

"Yeah, with a lousy record on fire safety." Jake retorted and Rose nodded sympathetically. Colin's plan to throw a barbeque on the field behind his house early in the summer, when the fire ban was already in place, had been the talk of the valley for weeks. Then once that was resolved, Jake and Colin had gone head to head over the latter's desire to burn off the field to clear it as a firebreak.

"You know, it's guys like him that make my job difficult. Nice people, but they just don't think." Jake's frustration was evident and the others nodded in agreement. Beside him water trickled down the side of the tender, and he looked round startled as he remembered why he was here. Quickly he pulled the hose out, detaching the connections and closing the tank.

"By the way Jake, before you go, you spent the morning at the Barnehursts fixing their fuse box. And they don't have any evacuees up there." Jim added as his brother gave a couple of experimental blasts to test the water spray.

"Thought not. I'll update my evacuation list." Jake nodded, obviously resigned to Roger's flexible ethics, as he hooked the mobile tender to the back of his car and headed off.

"So, what do we do?" Jill asked, watching Jake leave, and Matt shrugged.

"Can't build a fire break, can't fly out and take on the fire, can't have refugees here. Guess we wait."

"It'll be a long wait. There's at least another five hours until sundown," Rose commented, as the phone rang inside the hangar. As Matt wiped his grimy hands off, Jim vanished in to answer it, said a few sentences and came back out.

"That was Rob. He didn't have much time to talk, but he says he'll be staying down at Lakeside Airport once he's finished for the day. It's likely he's going to be flying too late to get back." Jim looked at Matt, who nodded. If his concern had been overwhelming before, he gave no sign of it now.

"How is he?" He might have been asking about the weather.

"Fine. Sounded a bit tired, but otherwise OK."

"How's the plane?" At Matt's question Jill started to chuckle, and Rose hid a smirk.

"I suppose we should be happy you asked after him first," Jill said, and Matt threw her a half-hearted scowl.

"Again, fine. Although he thinks one of the seats got slightly damaged." Jim paused as a dangerous silence fell and Matt turned to him with an enquiring glare. "I didn't get the details but he was trying to get a girl with a leg cast into the back seat and a metal part caught on the leather."

"I'll forgive him. This time." A rip in the leather was much easier to repair than his worried visions of a burning aircraft. Down at the Lakeside Airport, the private airport taken over as a base for the emergency services, the aeroplane was in good hands. Rob was definitely doing his bit against the fires, while his uncle just sat here feeling useless. Matt stared at his beer glumly. Coming to his own decision, he threw the remains of the drink back and stood up.

"Jim, you're a pilot. Want a quick run with me? Get some fly time in and spray down the valley entrance? A half hour or so won't break the bank." He threw a quick glance at Jill who shrugged.

"It's your money. You've never been good at sitting still have you?" she said, dryly.

"I thought you didn't fly when you'd been drinking?" Jim asked almost at the same time, even as he stood up with a grin.

"Why I'm asking another pilot to do the flying. I'll just advise." Without waiting for an answer, Matt headed across for the crop duster. The water tank was only half full, but he reckoned there was enough there for a quick flight. He began to disconnect the fuel hose first, turning off the fuel and letting the hose empty before he removed the connections to the plane. The crop sprayer would hardly need a full fuel tank for the short run to the end of the valley and back. Rose sauntered over, fascinated by anything mechanical, hands clasped firmly behind her back but watching closely.

"Done any crop spraying?" Matt asked Jim, as he worked. It was an idle check, but it always paid to make sure.

"No. I've flown single engine props before but not for that." Jim was looking the crop sprayer over, obviously trying to re-familiarise himself with the aircraft.

"Guess you usually fly something a bit bigger than this," Matt said, as he moved the fuel hose clear. He turned off the water at the tap, beginning to coil the spare length of hose round his arm as he walked back.

"Yeah. Four engines and a cargo hold capable of carrying a tank." Jim laughed slightly. "Believe me, I'm not going to miss the chance to get some flying time in on leave."

"Then you'd better start your walk round." Matt had finished coiling the water hose, pulling the end from the tank, and tossed the written checklist to him. Jim nodded and began following the list, Matt hovering to make sure he didn't miss anything. Finally, with both pilots satisfied, they took their seats. Matt settled himself awkwardly into the rear-facing mechanic's cabin as another pilot took his usual place at the front, reflecting it was a high price for an ill-timed beer. As Jim checked the controls and adjusted his seat Matt stayed quiet, trying not to distract him. It was not Jim's first time in the sprayer's cockpit, but it would be his first time flying her while she was actually spraying.

Once he was happy Jim had performed the pre-flight checks properly, Matt indicated he could start the engines up and turn onto the runway. Jill and Rose were well clear, heading down towards the house. He would worry about what they were cooking up later.

"Give her her head and she'll fly herself away," he said, once the engines had settled into a level note.

"Can't say that's a standard instruction," Jim muttered, as he increased throttle and the aircraft began to move. The mechanical buzz of the radial engine was a nice change from the smooth hum of the turbo props he was used to.

"With all the smoke aren't you worried about ash or heat clogging the engine?" Jim asked, as he manoeuvred her carefully into line for take-off. Facing down the runway he took a moment for one last check of the controls, and listened for other traffic on the local frequency.

He could hear none, not exactly a surprise when the smoke and heat were making flight conditions somewhat hazardous.

"Nah. We're miles from the ash, and she's got enough cooling to handle the heat," Matt replied. "Are you going to fly or talk?"

Jim scowled and announced his take off and flight intention over the radio, listening for any response. When there was none he began the take off, quickly remembering he had to keep the rudder hard over to compensate for the pull of the radial engine. Increasing throttle to full, he was surprised when the aircraft lifted after only a short distance, and kept her in a shallow climb.

"Half empty water tank helps," Matt spoke up from the back. "But she's got a pretty short run anyway."

"I'll remember that." The two fields at the end of the runway were passing under them, but with a steady climb Jim would be well above the tree line for the rise and the forest beyond it.

"Five passes. We'll do One-Three-Five-Two-Four. With last two passes, the edges of the previous runs will overlap." Matt sketched the pattern in the air with one finger even though

Jim could not see him. He was not a formal instructor, but then this wasn't an official lesson.

"To get extra coverage, right. But why not just turn her at the end of each and come back overlapping?" Jim asked, genuinely curious.

"Personal preference. If I've just been spraying chemicals, I don't like to fly through the cloud. Damages the paint, and it can be hell to get off the windscreen. Any other questions?"

"What's that taped there? Self destruct?" Jim pointed down, beside his seat, where a large flap of plastic had been sellotaped over a handle, as a makeshift cover. A large red "D" was scrawled on it. Immediately knowing what Jim was asking about, and safe in the knowledge that Jim could not see him, Matt grinned.

"Dump. If you pull it, it jettisons the contents of the water tank."

"To lighten the plane quickly in an emergency." Jim nodded in understanding.

"Yeah, but once it's pulled you can't stop or reset it until she's on the ground," Matt reproved, knowing that curious fingers had lifted the flap so their owner could peer underneath. "Just remember, the spray is start and stop. That's one use."

37

"'kay." They had flown out beyond the valley entrance, now at almost a thousand feet. Both pilots paused for a moment and stared. At this distance, the air above the fires danced and shimmered in a heat haze that ran across the sky. Only the plumes of smoke rising to form black and grey clouds showed where the individual fires were. As the winds drove the smoke clouds towards the valley, they could only hope that the flames below them would not follow.

Matt swallowed for a moment, trying not to think of Rob out there in the chaos. Jim obviously had similar thoughts.

"So, how does this spray work?" Jim asked, trying to divert the conversation back to their current flight. Matt collected himself.

"Usually you'd do it at fifteen feet above the fields." As Jim spluttered, Matt grinned wickedly. There was a small element of jealousy in his comment, as Matt well knew. He would have given his eye-teeth for a chance to fly the large four-engined military transports that were the younger pilot's bread and butter, and it was nice to have something he was better at. "But we won't ask you to do that, and treetops are a bit uneven. Drop to about two hundred feet and fly the pattern I showed you. I'll talk you through it."

Radioing his intent, in case anyone else was flying, Jim pulled a low turn and descended to bring himself at the right angle to fly across the valley entrance. As he approached, Matt settled himself more comfortably and began to issue instructions.

"Now's the best time. Turn the spray on. Straight ahead. Now turn right, little faster, good." Matt paused to let Jim finish his second run. "Now, turn left, not quite so hard, she's pretty responsive. Too far, don't worry, just correct. Good." The next run was completed to his satisfaction, but he knew what Jim had forgotten, simply from the way the aircraft was handling. "Turn the spray off. Don't forget your trim control. Wider curve to the left. You're aiming for the gap. Try to line up parallel to the big green trees." The big green trees – two large conifers towering above the forest – were a landmark known to all the Vale pilots. Positioned across the entrance to the Vale, forming a neat cross with the road, the two green trees in the middle of the gold forest were on the course they needed. Jim struggled slightly, and then Matt felt the aircraft lift away from the treetops.

"Sorry. I need to go around."

"Don't apologise for flying safe! Do a wider loop right round to the right and you can get back in position to get your approach lined up." Matt already knew his instructions were not necessary. Jim probably had more flying hours than he did, just not with this type of aviation. If Matt had not been confident in him as a pilot, he would never have let Jim near his beloved cockpit in the first place.

"Right." Jim said. "Lined up on the trees, approaching at two hundred feet, spray..." Matt waited as Jim paused.

"Turn it on," Matt confirmed and Jim did so, before he continued the pass, matching the crop sprayer's movements to his words.

"So we cross the valley at a steady two hundred feet and then turn left again, tighter turn to bring us back over this bit and then final pass to spray the bit we missed, and then finish and lift away." Jim completed his monologue proudly. A moment later he remembered to turn the spray off as Matt coughed from the back seat.

"So that's your first crop spray. Now you just need to keep doing that until you run out of fuel or water."

"Not funny."

"Just do one quick circle over the entrance, to spray the rest of the tank. You want her light to land." Jim followed instructions, and the white vapour trail formed behind them briefly before the water ran out.

"And that's it. Oh well, back to base." Matt scowled to himself. He had honestly thought he had more water in the tank than that. Still, every little helped. In the cockpit Jim complied, turning back towards the airfield.

"She's pretty agile. Not exactly stand on-your-wingtip flying, but still not bad." Jim nodded in general approval of the aircraft and Matt chuckled quietly.

"Land into the wind – north to south. There's fields for a run off if you do it in that direction. You'd be surprised. She's quite a mover. One thousand horsepower under the hood." Flying instructions first, chat second, at least as far as Matt was concerned.

"Gotcha. Is that why you bought a Dromader instead of a Thrush Commander?" Jim's mind was mainly on the airfield as he swung out over the valley to get a good approach.

"Adjust your trim. It was what was available, and it does the job. I'm not going to mess around with it if it works. Had to fix the intercom though. It'd be a boring flight if the poor sod in the back couldn't talk to the pilot." Matt sounded fairly blasé, but he was keeping an eye out for other traffic. At least one of the locals had a microlite and he did not trust them to be sensible enough to keep it on the ground in these conditions.

"Beginning approach to land at Brooke's Vale airstrip," Jim announced, and quickly and efficiently brought the aircraft down, in an excellent landing with virtually no bounce. At the end of the runway he turned it and began to taxi back to the hangar.

"Marks out of ten?"

"Lost the lot for being smug," Matt retorted. The landing had been perfect, and better than half of his.

"Beginner's luck," Jim replied, stopping the crop sprayer in her usual spot. "And by the way, your hangar's been domesticated."

Matt almost growled. Outside the hangar a small table had been set up, holding various plates of small triangular sandwiches, a tea set and coffee pot and as the final touch it was all resting on a red and white striped tablecloth. Jill sat beside it, holding a cup of tea and smiling urbanely.

"Don't laugh. Rose'll be doing this to you soon enough." Matt's comment showed he took no small amount of pleasure in the prospect. Jim laughed.

"Not a chance. But I might get back from a flight to find she's taken the car apart and laid the pieces out neatly on the lawn." With once in a lifetime timing, Rose chose that moment to walk out of the hangar, wiping her hands on a spare rag. Matt began to chuckle as he climbed out, and Jim smiled evilly.

"Just remember, your Shackleton's in that hangar." Jim tried not to laugh as for a moment Matt froze, and then walked purposefully towards the picnic table, throwing an anxious glance through the hangar doors as he went.

The power had not come back on, and Jill's impromptu picnic had been a spur of the moment decision to use up all the fresh food that was in danger of spoiling. Her reassurance that she had no intention of permanently civilising Matt's somewhat ramshackle hangar did a lot to calm ruffled feathers. Any lingering tensions vanished when she produced a plate of bacon, sausage and eggs from inside the hangar where Rose had carefully set up a small camping stove on the concrete floor, as Matt's stomach reminded him he had not eaten since this morning when Rob flew off.

"Any more of that for me?" Jim asked, hopefully. His attempt to nab a piece off Matt's plate was met with a dangerously raised fork, and a glare. Rose handed him another plate, and then vanished back inside to make sure the stove was turned off and cooling safely. Returning with a third plate, she sat down and tucked in.

"So, how was the flight?"

"Not bad." Jim nodded, and settled down to the dirty details. Matt assisted with an occasional grunt but was generally paying attention to his food, which was vanishing at quite an alarming rate. As they finished the cooked food the conversation began to peter out. Without meaning to, gradually eyes turned towards the far horizon where the sun was now low in the sky. Shining scarlet through the clouds, there was a disturbing shimmer around it as the heat haze rose. Odd comments could not break the glum mood, and Matt found himself wondering again how Rob was doing out there.

The sound of an engine alerted them to someone coming up the road, providing a grateful distraction. After some peering confirmed it was Jake, Jill quickly added another crate to serve as a makeshift chair. It was not until the car pulled up, covered to its windows in dust and with grass caked onto its wheel wells, that they realised something was wrong.

Jake climbed out, slamming the car door. He was in a state, soaked in sweat, covered in the brown dry dust of the valley from head to foot, and obviously exhausted. He leaned against the car for a moment before he walked across, shaking his head.

"Mind if I hook the tender up for a refill?" Jake asked, surprisingly mildly. The others had stood up as he arrived, taking in his disheveled appearance. Matt and Jim exchanged a quick glance, and then Matt turned and vanished into the hangar without a word.

"No problem," Jim replied, over the sound of Matt digging out another hose. "You'll need to park next to the pump again though.

Take the Robin's usual spot."

For a few moments there was a quick bustle of industry as Matt and Rose connected the longer hose to the water store while Jim and Jake moved the car and got everything hooked up. Once the reassuring sound of water flowing had begun and the tender was quickly filling, Jake bent over nearly double to catch his breath.

"What happened?" Jim asked, worried. He put a hand on his brother's shoulder, and Jake straightened, shaking him off.

"Stupid blasted kids. Mind if I grab a chair?" Without waiting for an answer he walked across, a little more slowly than usual, and took the seat that Matt gestured to. Pouring himself a mug of strong black coffee he downed most of it and paused, obviously collecting his thoughts. The others did not press him, and once he had recovered slightly he began.

"Nick's refugees. The kids got bored and decided to amuse themselves." He took a breath obviously struggling to keep his tone level. "Starting fires with a magnifying glass on that field out the back. Don't worry, Nick caught them early and between his hose and my tender we've put everything out and soaked the field down."

"No." Rose shook her head in disbelief. In this climate the sheer stupidity of the action was hard to believe.

"Yep. They were lighting bits of paper to watch them burn. Of course when the wind took them they didn't bother to chase them down. I've just spent the last two hours walking round Nick's field making sure the fire they started is out, and nothing's quietly smoldering. Even with Nick's help that's a big job."

"I've some whisky in the house," Matt volunteered, but Jake shook his head.

"I'd rather keep my head clear until they're gone. Just in case they do it again."

"Nick must be livid," Jill remarked, looking across the valley to the field.

"Absolutely furious. They've been politely invited to get their stuff and leave, refugees or no."

"I'm surprised he's not pressing charges." Rose shook her head again, still stunned that anyone would light a fire in the middle of a fire ban.

"If he doesn't, and they don't leave, I will. One way or another I want them out. You've got me to mind the whole valley on my own, and those kids just became a fire risk."

47

Jake had calmed down slightly. "Their parents were appalled, so they were relieved when I gave them the option to get out instead of pressing charges. They'll be gone as soon as they're packed."

As Jake finished Jill pushed a plate of sandwiches at him and he grabbed one. It was gone in two bites.

"Help yourself to the rest. I'm afraid you missed dinner."

"Thanks. I'm starving. And I've got another problem." Jake shifted uncomfortably. "Matt, how much fuel do you have in that tank?"

"Enough for a couple of months." Matt looked him straight in the eye, but said nothing more, forcing Jake to continue.

"Yeah. In strict interpretation, under these circumstances, it's a fire risk."

"Are you telling me to dump my fuel?" Matt's voice stayed very level.

"I'm warning you it might be a possibility. I'll need to contact headquarters to see what they want to do to make it safe. Sorry, mate." Jake looked down awkwardly. He liked Matt, but he had a job to do.

"After a close shave like the kids, I can

understand. But I'll need compensation."

"I'll see what I can do," Jake promised, nodding. He finished off the remains of the sandwiches, and nodded at Jill. "Nice. I think I'll head home."

"I'll drive. Leave the water tender up here, it'll be filled by the morning." Jim looked his brother over and placed himself firmly by the driver's door of the car, preventing Jake from getting in.

"That's fine here." Matt nodded at the tender. He'd seen Jake stumble as he stood up, and was quite glad that Jim had stopped him before Matt could.

"Fine." Jake was obviously too tired to argue and climbed into Jim's car gratefully. The mood of the evening had been broken, and as Jake and Jim left, Jill said her goodbyes and headed off with Rose. Obviously the two had something they were planning, as Matt heard the name Roger mentioned briefly.

He turned back to the runway, ignoring the water tender as it steadily filled, and looked over the aircraft in its usual parking spot. The Dromader was a crop sprayer, not a water-bomber, but it carried almost two thousand litres fully loaded. It was not enough to soak down the entire valley, but he could get to trouble spots faster and drop more water than Jake's mobile tender.

He was not going to argue the case with the exhausted fire marshal, but dumping fuel, or even moving it out of the valley by plane or road, was completely impractical. He was not sure if Jake realised how much fuel he had stored, but the Shackleton's engine tests used a lot. The tank was nearly full. However, if he could get compensation for disposing of the fuel, that opened up options outside the valley, not least flying some of it off. After all, if Nick was right and other crop sprayers were already helping with the fires, surely there had to be something he could do. He sat back, turning the possibilities over in his mind until the tender had filled and he could turn the water off.

Distracted, he closed the hangar up for the night even though the Robin, the only aircraft that really needed the protection, was absent and walked slowly back to the house. The sun set behind him, blood red in a cloudy sky.

Day One

"That was the Emergency Services on the phone. They say you need to dispose of your fuel." At eight o'clock sharp Jill walked across from the mobile office by the hangar where she had spent the morning. The news she brought was not unexpected.

The day had brightened, rather than dawned. The wind was pulling the smoke towards the Vale, and streamers of it marked the otherwise blue sky. A red swollen sun was vaguely visible through the sky full of ash, and the clouds loomed ominously over the horizon.

53

Despite the fire crews' efforts the fire front had moved and grown overnight. Rob had phoned at six to let Matt know he had been asked to continue flying evacuations to Lakeside as more houses were threatened. After a brief admonishment to fly safe and not damage his plane, Matt had given his permission. Now Jill's news meant the airstrip itself would be affected.

"How?" Matt asked abruptly, and Jill blinked. "There's nowhere to dump it around here where it won't get into the ground or the fire."

"They just said it can't stay this close to the town." Jill shrugged helplessly. "If it matters they said that the cost would be covered."

Slowly and unexpectedly a smile spread across Matt's face. He looked at his fuel store, and then the crop sprayer, and the grin grew wider. The call had come at exactly the right time as far as Matt was concerned. The morning haze had lifted and the sky was clear enough for reasonable flying condition. Privately, he was also grateful that it had come after Jake left to investigate the hopefully false alarm at the Sampsons. The fire marshal was likely to be a lot more resistant to his plans, if only because with

Rob already flying Jake would not want another friend at risk.

"So we need to get rid of my season's store of fuel. And my crop sprayer's got a two thousand litre water tank." He looked at their stunned faces and started to laugh. "Water, you muppets. How much of the area can we soak if fuel's no object? Well? Get cracking!"

His words broke the spell. Rose and Jill dashed out to get the pump set up, while Jim and Matt began to check the plane over. They connected the hoses to water and fuel and slowly the plane began to refuel while the water tank filled. An hour later and the aircraft was ready.

He waved them away from the crop sprayer and began his walk round. The plane had been out on the runway overnight and between birds, wildlife, ash and accidents, it was as well to make sure the plane was in flying condition before you got into it. Satisfied, Matt climbed into the cockpit, and Jim waved him off, before he jumped into his car to head for town. There was at least one decent water pump he could think of, and the more quickly they could get water into the crop sprayer the better.

Matt pointed the aircraft down the runway, clicked on the radio and announced his intended course in case of other traffic in the area. He did not hear any on the standard channels and began his take off run. The aircraft accelerated faster than usual, as her pilot tried to ignore the small voice of sanity in the back of his head, which was protesting the whole idea. After all, his crop duster might get sooty.

He chuckled to himself, aware there was no one to hear him, and turned the aircraft south. The old Rookery Hunting Lodge was only a few minutes flight out of town, but with its carefully maintained lawns and woodland, it was an obvious target. It had also been evacuated early, so there was no one to see it if he messed up. He looked down at the forest below him and shook his head. All browns and golds as far as he could see, even the pine trees. He preferred the rich green of the live woodlands. This looked like a tinderbox waiting for a match.

He radioed his intent again and banked the plane, lining her up for a long low run along the edge of the woods. Usually he would be at almost head height over fields, but forests were trickier. Less uniform, he had to worry about the occasional tall tree, or a bird flying up and into his path. He settled on a height he was happy with and hoped he had guessed correctly.

Nervous, even though he would never admit it, he pulled the plane into a shallow dive. As he levelled her out, a scant twenty feet above the tree line, he hit the spray. He didn't bother to turn it off as he banked and turned for a second parallel run, treating the woods as an exceptionally large field. It didn't matter where the water went, as long as the forest was soaked. Matt repeated this for a few more runs, until the tank was empty and sat back with a smile. That should help.

When he looked back, his heart sank. Even as he turned for home, he could not tell which parts of the forest he had sprayed and which he had not. While he had expected the wet leaves to show darker against the yellow forest, the parched earth had simply absorbed the water as he sprayed it. With the sun beating down relentlessly he wondered how much had simply evaporated. Matt blinked at the scale of the task he had set himself, and wondered why he had ever thought this would work. When the fire service with their Canadairs and Antonovs could not do it, expecting one crop sprayer to make a difference was obviously unreasonable. Even so, he knew he would still be filling the crop duster up and flying out again. Perhaps, he admitted privately, it was simply because he could not live with himself if he sat back and did nothing. Chuckling aloud, he turned and headed back for the next load.

On arrival there was some good news. Rose was standing by the bay holding a large black hose and connector, and a power cord trailed from his reserve batteries to the pump by the well. Both had been carefully fastened down clear of the runway and bays. Jim walked across and climbed up, sticking his head in the cockpit window.

"Mind if you move her across a bit? Your water tank's stuck, so we've got the pump set up for the well to connect straight to your tank."

As he followed the directions, Matt rolled the crop sprayer into place. Jim fitted the fuel nozzle, while Rose quickly attached the water and turned the pump on. The way they had set it up was simple and quick.

"She doesn't need that much fuel," Matt advised, and Rose nodded.

"I'll top off the tank anyway. Jim, are you going to refuel the pilot?" She grinned as Jim took Matt's arm, leading him firmly into the hangar. The kettle would be boiling about now, since Jill had put it on when they heard the aircraft returning.

Inside the hangar, Jim shoved a large mug of coffee at Matt. The older man sat down heavily, legs betraying him slightly. What he had done was not, in itself particularly difficult, but the fact it was his first fire-fighting flight seemed to have got to him. He sniffed at the mug and looked at Jim suspiciously.

"It's just coffee. I know your views on beer when flying," Jim said, and paused to let Matt take a testing sip. "So, how was it?"

"Dead loss," Matt replied sardonically, and threw back the brew despite the steam rising off it. "Too much area to cover and too dry. It soaked in as I sprayed it." The answer was cutting, but his tone was angry, not defeated.

"So you won't be flying out again, then?" Jim sat down, sounding disappointed.

"Course I will." Matt laughed sourly and Jim nodded, choosing his words with care.

Matt could be prideful and, as they all knew, ideas needed to be put to him in the right way.

"I had a word with Jake. He's still got a few friends on the force, and he knows the fire chief. Of course, they would never usually ask for help from civilians, but under the circumstances they are very short handed." Jim was not exactly truthful about the conversation with Jake. He had not asked him specifically about using the crop sprayer to help, convinced the answer would be an outright refusal. Instead he had carefully asked about the best areas to spray for firebreaks behind the lines.

"And what do they want me to do about it?" Matt growled, trying to hide his interest. Jim pointed at the map he had laid out on the floor, hiding his smile poorly.

"Here. The fires here and here are small ones, and they've pulled back because they haven't enough men. They think they will burn themselves out, but there is a risk of them spreading. If you can soak here and here thoroughly, it will help contain them." Jim looked up at the sudden noise. Matt was drumming his fingers on the box he was sitting on, looking at the hangar wall as he concentrated. Suddenly he swung back to Jim and pointed at the map.

"So the more water I can get here and here the better? Sounds simple. Choose one and wake me up when the plane's ready." With that Matt's head lolled back against the hangar wall and his eyes closed. Jim gave him a moment, and then went outside to check on the plane. He hoped he had imagined the old crop duster's hands shaking.

There was not really much to do now, except wait, the smoke on the breeze drowned out by the stink of grease from the electric fuel pump. On a whim Jim checked the reserve charge in the battery but that was quite adequate. The wind that was driving the fire towards them was also driving the turbine to create all the power they needed. Then he checked the water stores, only to find that Jill had already thoughtfully filled sets of spare bottles from the mains just in case. Rose was fiddling with something on the side of Matt's large water tank, which usually only held rainwater, not good enough to drink but fine for washing the planes down and watering the grass. After the long dry season, it was almost empty and from what he could tell between her swearing and the occasional metallic screech the spigot had stuck closed. Jim fidgeted, watching the road. He really needed to speak to Jake about the fuel issue, but his brother had been up at the Sampsons for a couple of hours. Hopefully it was not anything serious. Time passed, and he drummed his fingers impatiently. Rose emerged from under the water tank, victorious, only to open the spigot and have a drain of brown foul-smelling liquid emerge.

"What did you expect? It's been half empty all summer." His chuckle definitely did not improve her mood.

"I thought we could fill it from the well and keep it as a backup, just in case we need to spray down the valley and the water's out." Rose sounded disappointed, but Jim paused and looked at her innocent expression. He suspected they had exactly the same goal in mind for the crop sprayer, but to make it work they would need access to an awful lot of water.

With typical timing that was when he realised Jake's car was on its way back, towing the water tender behind it. The drone of the fuel pump and clangs and screeches from Rose's project had drowned out the engine until it was quite close, and now the small car was making its way up to the airfield. Jim mentally ran through his approach, knowing that his brother was going to be hard to sell on his idea, but also that there were other concerns taking precedence.

This time the car was in decent condition and when Jake climbed out, he looked surprisingly happy.

"What was up at the Sampsons?" Jim asked the important question first, as his brother shut the car door.

"False alarm. They reported something bright and orange moving, but no smoke. What they actually saw was this." Jake grinned and held up a shredded piece of torn brilliant orange fabric. "Off a high-visibility jacket, I think. It was caught on a bush, and fluttering in the wind it looked like a fire. Took long enough to find it and confirm there weren't any other fires. I think the kids yesterday were a bit of a wake-up call, but at least they're taking it seriously."

"Any news overnight?" Rose asked, and he frowned.

"Not good. Some of the fire fronts have joined up. Either there's a bunch of firebugs out there, or the fire just keeps breaking through. It's bad news for Matt. I've been asked to make sure he's removing his fuel. He has been told, right?" He looked at them suspiciously, aware that Matt's bad temper was legendary.

"He knows." Jim threw a sidelong glance at Rose, uncertain what to say.

"Don't tell me he refused." Jake sighed, rubbing a hand across his face. He could not remember the safety limits of Matt's tank off-hand but if it ruptured burning avgas in a forest fire, let alone in the restricted confines of the valley, would be a nightmare.

"No." Jim hedged slightly, uncertain of the best way to break their idea to his brother. Jake had always been the practical one.

"Is that why he took the crop sprayer up? Don't look so surprised, I saw it coming in to land while I was on my way back here."

"Well yeah, he was getting rid of fuel. But there's a problem." Jim knew he was dancing around the issue, and could not think of how to approach it.

"He's got quite a lot of fuel." Rose cut to the point.

"How much fuel has he got?" Jake asked, trying to gauge the scope of the problem.

"Almost two thousand gallons in the underground tank. In the light aircraft, about forty to fifty hours running time." Jim replied, grateful that his girlfriend had given him an opening.

"And in the Shack?" Jake was joking, but Jim shrugged.

"Maybe two or three hours, if you were lucky."

"You're kidding." As Jim opened his mouth to protest, Jake waved it shut. "I'll take your word on it. That's going to be hard to dispose of."

"You could always let him fly it off." Jim made the suggestion as casually as he could.

"Sorry?" Jake's comment was a request for clarity, and his disbelieving tone was not promising.

"The crop sprayer carries two thousand litres of water. If Matt sprayed down some of the isolated houses or fields it reduces the risk of fire," Jim said. "Simple flying for a crop sprayer pilot like him."

"How are you going to get water? Two thousand litres is what, four or five hundred gallons? That's a lot to pull from the mains, even assuming they don't go out." Jake's words seemed more testing than outright rejection.

"The well."

"That's not clean water. Pull it at the wrong time you'll get a mouthful of salt."

"I don't think the fire cares."

"The aquifer refills it on each high tide, so it won't run out." Rose reminded him.

"But if it runs dry between the tides, the only other well's in town."

"So while the aircraft is flying we drive your tender and a couple of cans down, fill them and then when the plane comes back we stick the hose in and refill the tank. Then we top her off directly from the mains. We could probably get her refilled in less than an hour." Rose replied, and Jim nodded in agreement.

Jake thought it through slowly. He had thought there would be less fuel at the end of season, but two thousand gallons would take a tanker to move and the forest fire made transporting avgas by road highly dangerous. If he agreed to them flying it off then the airport would always be manned, so problems or fires could be tackled early.

His main concern was that the crop sprayer could not refill for more than one or two flights a day, if that. Dedicated water bombers could refill in minutes and often carried several times the load, but on reflection if the crop sprayer could take on preventative duties that would free the larger aircraft to tackle the blazes directly. Slowly he nodded, coming to a decision. Looking round for Matt he saw the pilot standing by the crop sprayer while it refuelled. He walked across, trailed by Rose and Jim who were not being left behind at this point.

"What's this Jim was saying about fire fighting?" he asked, cutting straight to the point.

"You asked me to dispose of the fuel."

"So why can't you dump it?" Jake already knew the answer, but he wanted to make sure all the options had been explored. He was, after all, the one who would have to justify any unusual suggestions.

"Where?" Matt smiled slightly as Jake paused. The safest place for the fuel in the valley was the underground tank it would be dumped out of. Unfortunately, after what he had learned from the authorities, Jake knew that was not safe enough. He was not easily deterred however.

"Why not put it in the monster in your hangar and burn it off?"

"Griffon engines blow sparkplugs and catch fire," Matt replied calmly. "Notorious for it. That's a fire risk."

"Where's the fuel safer, Jake? In an underground tank or sitting in a rusty plane in hot sunlight?" Jim interrupted. His smirk vanished as they both rounded on him, Jake's demand for family loyalty coming at exactly the same time as Matt's furious protest that none of his planes were rusty. There was a very fraught moment, and then Jim turned on his heel and left them to it, shaking his head as he ducked round the plane to check on the connections.

"Look, I've had a good few years dumping liquid on the landscape. She might not be a water bomber, but she holds two thousand litres. That's got to be some use." Matt's statement was as close to a plea that he be allowed to help as his pride would let him utter. Jake looked thoughtful, considering the offer. With no way to get a tanker up here to move the fuel, and a capped tank still vulnerable to extreme heat or human vandals, it seemed increasingly like the best option.

"What's your flight experience?" he asked carefully. "Be precise."

"I've been crop dusting for ten years. Over eight thousand hours flying various types. Two thousand in the Drom."

"OK, let me have a word. No promises." Jake strode off towards the house, and behind him Matt frowned. He had expected his offer to be rejected outright, as he had with the Robin. The fact it was not raised a nagging worry that the situation outside the valley was worse than they knew.

As Jake reached the house the door opened and Jill stepped out. She spared a glance at the glowering fire marshal, nodding a quick greeting, before she dismissed him and walked up to Matt. She was holding his large map book closed round one finger, and opened it as she reached the bay.

"Matt, your next job." Jill was grinning a little too widely, and when Matt saw where she was pointing on the map he scowled.

"Very funny."

"No joke. Since they can't move the livestock, Nate and his crew are staying to protect them. At least you know the farm well."

"Hope Nate won't think he gets his next sprays for free as well," Matt grumbled. He had known the old farmer for years and counted him as one of his most valued customers.

Before this the fire had been a remote threat, something that always had to be handled at the end of the summer season. Now it was affecting not just people he knew, but also his business, and somehow it seemed a more immediate danger. He scanned the areas on the map Jill pointed to, and nodded.

"Jim?" he asked without looking up.

"She's refuelled and ready for your walk round," the younger pilot said, stepping away. With a grunted acknowledgement, Matt went across to examine his plane.

"You sure about flying this?" Jim asked. He was watching Matt closely for any sign of the tremors he had seen earlier.

"Yeah. Might ask you to take over for the afternoon." Matt paused for a moment. The tone was matter-of-fact, with no sign of any toll it had taken on his pride. Jim nodded, offering the other pilot a graceful way out.

"If we swap over we can spell each other. That way we both get a break from the smoke." He made the suggestion and was relieved when Matt nodded more cheerfully.

"I'd better go before Jake can stop me then." The crop sprayer pilot continued the pre-flight checks while Jill, finding herself ignored, went back to the house and the radio scanner.

Matt reminded himself not to rush, while at the same time half expecting an indignant fire marshal to storm out of the house, demanding they drain the fuel out of the plane and cap the ground tank off. Finally, mercifully, the checks were complete and Matt eagerly started the engine. A few moments later the crop sprayer was a yellow dot receding into the distance.

Jim watched him take-off and then wandered into the hangar. There was not really anything he could do until the plane came back. With everything ready for the crop sprayer's return and Jake on the phone to the powers-that-be, Jim found himself at a loose end, a pilot without a plane. Ignoring the coffee he looked at the large shape set back in the shadows, the familiar blunt nose turned towards him. It brought back a few memories and slowly he began to meander round the plane, in a brief stroll that quickly turned into a thorough inspection of Matt's handiwork. He had to admit that Matt had done a good job on it, restoring it with the same meticulous attention he spent on his flying aircraft. The Shackleton had been little more than rivets and rust when it arrived, but two years later it was almost unrecognisable. All the surface corrosion had been carefully removed, new hydraulics and pipes added, and Matt had even gone to the trouble of painting her in the gunmetal grey livery of her active duty years.

Out of habit Jim avoided the propellers, even if they were stationary. Hard to see in the dark, the thirteen-foot blades could give an unwary visitor quite a wallop if they walked into them.. Instead he walked under the long glider-like wing section beyond the outer engine and round to the door in the side of the fuselage. He knew that Matt was still working on the inside, but he was curious. Thoughtfully Matt had left the door open and a ladder in place. Jim could not resist. He was halfway up the ladder when a polite cough let him know he was not alone.

"If Matt catches you messing around with that plane, you're in for it." Rose observed from behind him.

"He won't mind." Jim twisted round to try to get a look at her. Stuck halfway up a ladder, part way into someone else's aeroplane was not the most innocent or dignified position for her to catch him in. She had to have done it deliberately, he decided, because the timing was just too good. Carefully, he backed down the ladder and turned to face her before he finished answering. "As I was saying, he won't mind. Who do you think helps him with the welding?"

"Really?" Rose's expression did not change, but the tone said everything.

"Yes. Of course, if he caught me working on it without his consent..." He stopped and let the silence speak for itself as her lips started to twitch.

"He would be unhappy?" she asked archly, and he nodded, hanging his head in mock shame. He wandered back to the coffee and sat down, holding the kettle up in mute enquiry. She nodded and he poured a couple of mugs.

"Why so interested in it? It's not exactly a pretty plane, but you've been up here whenever you have time free." Rose sipped at her coffee, as she waited for an answer. It was a question that had been on her mind for a while, and Jim mulled it over for a while before telling her the truth.

"I almost bought it," he said, and watched the shocked expression on his girlfriend's face with some pleasure. He knew he would not be allowed to leave it there, and sat back getting comfortable. Rose recognised the signs of a long story and did the same.

"I used to fly them, right at the end of their service. Fourteen hour long maritime patrols, looking out for trouble, search and rescue, anything that relieved the tedium for a while."

"Some of the patrol guys would do stupid things, daredevil risks to pass the time. Others – well there are a few reports of them tormenting the navy vessels out there. I'm odd, I guess, but I spent so long in the blasted things I miss them. When this airframe came up for auction on retirement I put in a sealed bid." He chuckled. "Don't know what I was thinking, my back pay was nowhere near enough, and I had nowhere to put her anyway."

"And then you found out Matt had bought it?"

"Yep. I think he found out it was up for auction from Jake, who was trying to stop me doing something stupid, but I've never asked. He certainly doesn't know I used to fly them."

"Why not tell him?"

"Because I used to fly this one." Jim chuckled, watching Rose's expression change as she worked it out. "You know what he's like. I'd never be allowed near it again just in case I made off with it."

"What, you think you could actually make it fly?"

"Not a chance. She's actually a bit too heavy, even if the runway was long enough, and she's missing two engines." Rose looked confused and Jim stood up, gesturing her across to the side of the aircraft.

"See up there? The back of the outer engines? She's supposed to have six engines. The Mark 3 were too heavy to take off fully loaded, so they added two extra Viper jet engines on the back of those engines just to get her into the air. Once she's up, she's fine. This one doesn't have the workings. Either they were missing on delivery or Matt removed them because they were too badly corroded. Probably the latter, but then flying over seawater will do that." He stopped his lecture, aware that Rose had quietly begun to snigger. "What's so funny?"

"Nothing. Sorry but speaking as an engineer, that's a hell of a design flaw. Too heavy to fly on its own engines."

"It just needed a little boost," Jim said, surprised at how defensive he still felt about the aircraft, even though he did not own it. "And one of these days I'm going to get you up in a plane."

"Not likely. I'm a nervous flyer. Not terrified, just nervous." She shifted at the disbelieving expression on his face.

"And yet you're dating me?"

"And I'll happily wave goodbye and wait for you on the ground as you fly off into the sunset, thank you very much." She planted her feet firmly on the ground and gave him a sweet smile.

"Anyway, shouldn't you be helping Jill on the radio?" Jim asked, trying to change the subject, and Rose's reaction surprised him. She looked away uncomfortably.

"I'm letting it cool down a bit in there before I head back in. After Jake left, we had words."

"Oh?"

"She asked a few questions about us, and our plans. I think she was trying to distract herself from the fire and Matt." Rose shifted position, looking up from her linked hands. "I'm afraid I told her that when half the next county's on fire, Matt's flying with the emergency services and you might be going up next, it wasn't a good time to discuss relationships." Jim shook his head, rolling his eyes. The course of their three-year romance had been disrupted frequently by his deployments and her studies. As a result, it seemed to be one of the locals' favourite topics of conversation, much to the dismay of Rose's grandmother. The grand dame prefered to pretend he did not exist.

"What a time to bring that up. Why don't you just tell Jill I'll propose the same day I get to fly you?" Jim said, inwardly grateful that he was not the one getting the questions.

"Why, so she can knock me on the head and bundle me into the back seat of the Robin?" Rose chuckled and Jim grinned at her.

"Well, if Jake's in town, then I should head out. It's my brotherly duty to give him a hand – and do some extra lobbying on Matt's behalf. Want to come?" he suggested, and Rose caught on instantly.

"And give Jill a chance to simmer down? Let's go. Although you get to tell her we're leaving."

Matt flew back, grinning to himself in the knowledge of a job well done. Nate's farm was not the easiest to spray, all rolling hills and awkward angles, but he had been working it for years. Spraying the hillsides so the channels and ditches filled from the run-off was relatively simple.

A neat approach and landing, polished by many years practice, brought him back to the Brooke's Vale airstrip. Then he saw the group, his informal flying club, standing by the hangar ahead of him and stopped the engine early. Although they were all sensible around aircraft he preferred not to taxi with people anywhere near the runway, after the near miss last year when a evacuee's child had made his way onto the airfield. Instead he climbed out and walked across, leaving the crop sprayer partway down the tarmac. If Rose, Jill, Jim and Jake were all waiting like that it probably meant there was something important to tell him, hopefully good news.

"Went well out there?" Jim greeted Matt as he approached.

"Yeah. All done." Matt was not really paying attention to the other pilot. Instead he was watching Jake carefully. Unfortunately, the fire marshal's poker face was excellent.

"Confident flying these conditions?" Jake asked. Matt nodded, equally as casual.

"Definitely."

"I heard back from the Emergency Services. If you're going to keep flying out there, it would be useful if you did it as part of a concerted effort, rather than out on your own." Jake's tone was completely professional.

"So what would I have to do?" Matt already knew he would agree, but he was too contrary to accept anything without a protest. It was the principle of the thing. Jake looked at Jill, who grinned at Matt and held up a notepad.

"When you're flying, use this frequency unless instructed otherwise. It's the one they use to co-ordinate air traffic. I've let them know we've got two pilots, as they were a bit concerned about the hours you would be flying." Jill was drawing it out deliberately to lure him in, without realising this offer was exactly what Matt had been hoping for. Usually, once she had his interest, she needed to get him to take the bait. This time he did not disappoint her.

"And?"

"You'd have your own assigned call sign. C-SPRY 10."

"Seaspray?" He pronounced it phonetically, and his mouth quirked. "I like that."

"C-SPRY 10," she corrected. "C-SPRY is the tag they're using for all the crop sprayers on duty."

"Jim, whaddya think?" Matt's lopsided grin was met by Jim's. "Does she look like a Seaspray to you?"

"I think C-SPRY 10 is in business." Jim replied.

"There are a few things we'll need to get sorted out here. We need a radio receiver, which you have, but also a way to call them back." Jill began, looking at the list she was holding.

"My radios are in the planes, but there's a landline in the house." Matt suggested, and Jim nodded.

"We've also left most of our mobiles in there, in case the phones go out." He gave Matt a semi-apologetic glance.

"Setting this up without me, were you?" Matt asked, without real ire.

"You ungrateful wretch." Jim's laugh took the sting out of his words. "Were you going to say no? After I spent an hour persuading them that you were qualified for more than a pension?" Matt glared at him. Jill cleared her throat to get their attention and continued.

"C-SPRY 10 officially has two pilots, Matt, you're the primary, and Jim is the fallback. It's an hours issue apparently. They'll do most of the call-ins and mission planning here, so it's ready for the pilots. Once you're up you take directions over the radio. It's a busy channel so listen for your call-sign carefully. Any problems?" Jim, who already knew most of this, nodded. Matt thought about it briefly and then did the same.

"Fine. Whoever's not flying gets to help out with the planning. I don't want junior here damaging my aircraft by trying something he's not capable of." Matt shot the other pilot a superior stare, and Jim flinched, clutching his hands theatrically over his chest.

"Thanks for the vote of no-confidence."

"Anytime."

"Is that everything?" The edge to Jill's tone reminded them that she was still trying to arrange the details. There were a pair of sheepish nods. "Great. I'll let them know. Jake, looks like we're on." She turned and vanished into the house. Rose headed towards the fuel tank to get the hoses ready as Matt walked back to the plane to move it the remaining distance down the runway. As the engine started it covered the conversation of the twins, standing by the hangar.

"How'd you swing this, Jake?" Jim was watching the other two as they worked, but wanted the question answered first.

"I didn't." His brother's face was drawn. "He's got more experience than half the pilots they've got up there. They pretty much bit my hand off when I asked."

"What's going on?" Jim asked quietly, serious for once and Jake looked round quickly, making sure the others were not in hearing before he answered.

"This is off the record and completely confidential." Jim nodded and his brother's voice dropped even lower. "One of the official spray company airfields went up early on. They suspect arson. Several of the planes were lost or damaged. Then another one got hit. Possibly deliberately."

"Arson? But –"

"Accidents don't take crowbars to capped fuel tanks."

"Oh shit. Is that why they were so concerned about the fuel by Brooke's Vale?" Jim's stunned comment brought a dry chuckle from his brother.

"Probably. They're flying in replacements, but it all takes time. With the airfields out they've got to arrange places for the planes to set down. Meanwhile every little helps. Don't expect to be taking on the fire directly – the remaining experienced pilots are doing that. Your job's to damp down the fields, help with the firebreaks, etc. And keep the airfield occupied, just in case." As he heard Jake's explanation, Jim nodded slowly.

"Makes sense. I suppose we'd better help the others with the plane then."

The refuelling time dragged. It was only an hour, but it seemed longer. Matt checked the crop sprayer over twice, paced around the hangar and eventually settled on sitting by the coffee pot glaring at anyone who came near.

Since Rose and Jim were used to this behaviour during the crop-spraying season, it had very limited effect. Jake had excused himself early and gone to check round the valley again, while Jill was sitting by the radio getting set up for their new official role. Finally their patience was rewarded as she walked out of the house clutching the map book and a sheet of notes. The others clustered quickly round the coffee, waiting to hear what she had to say.

"Right, Matt, your first official mission is this homestead. It's near to one of the smaller fires, and the residents stayed to try and save their house. The firemen have contained the main blaze, but apparently the residents are having problems with hot ash starting smaller blazes near their home. If you can soak the area, it will help." Jill pointed them out on the map, and Matt nodded.

"That's about forty minutes each way, more if we allow for turbulence," he said.

"So if we expect you out for two hours?" Jill queried, and Matt nodded.

"Yeah. You've got the radio scanner, so keep listening. I'll signal if anything goes wrong."

"How long until you can leave?"

"Give it ten minutes to finish my walk round." Matt swung round and glared at Jim, who had muttered the words 'his third'. "Thoroughness around aircraft is always essential."

"Yessir." Jim's riposte earned him a curled lip and disdainful glance from Matt, who finished his drink, stood up and went over to the crop sprayer.

"I think that means we're dismissed." Rose folded her arms with a grin and Jill nodded.

"I'll let them know what the plans are then. Somehow I don't think Matt's going to wait for me to get back before he takes off, is he?" As Jill went back to the house, Jim watched the older pilot give each tyre a good hard kick, and had to agree with her.

Matt enjoyed flying, and liked to be useful, so the chance to do both at once was rare and very welcome. The take off had been uneventful, and now he was cruising towards his first official target.

As he passed Lydford, the queue of cars evacuating reminded him of why he was doing this. He wondered how many of them would be stopping at the Vale for food and supplies before they headed on to wherever they were bound. It was a sobering thought that Lydford needed evacuation. It had only happened a handful of times in his memory, and usually meant the fires were serious. However, that was not his target.

Instead he carried on, out to the west where he knew the homestead was. The owners had elected to stay to fight the fire and, although it was one of the smaller blazes that threatened them, any help would be useful.

He swallowed, suddenly struck by doubts. Should he spray down the farmstead or the fire itself? If he put too much water on the house roof, would it collapse? What kind of turbulence would the fire create? What height would it be safe to spray from? How well would the crop sprayer handle the heat? How many passes could he manage? What had seemed so simple on the ground suddenly seemed almost unbelievably complex, an easy task suddenly turned into a daunting prospect. Matt steadied himself. He had wanted a chance to help and now he had got it. All he could do was his best, and hope it was enough.

He was in the area now, looking below him for any sign of a building or clear land in the forest. As he caught a glimpse of one, he snatched a glance at the map beside him. It looked like the right place. So far so good. Matt lined up to over fly the house and get an idea of the situation before he planned his route, putting the aircraft into a shallow dive for a low pass.

The cabin abruptly filled with eye-watering smoke. Coughing and taken by surprise Matt threw the crop sprayer into a climb, banking and turning to get away from the irritation. As quickly as it came, he was through it and the cabin cleared, leaving only the faint acrid smell of smoke. The wind was blowing towards the house, driving the fire in that direction, but ahead of the blaze it carried the smoke and ash. He cursed himself for an idiot; if the smoke could be smelled at Brooke's Vale it would obviously be much worse up close, and even thicker above the fire.

He turned in a wide circle to view the situation, trying to keep clear of the ash. On the hillside below, a large expanse of land had been cleared, the stubble ploughed in to the ground to make a firebreak. Even on that bare earth he could see small smoke plumes rising where the ash settled, indicating it had been a rushed job and less than thorough. Worse was the house itself where, from its dusty brown roof, small curls of smoke had begun to rise and thicken.

Matt had not got a scarf onboard – in the height of summer it was unlikely to be needed. With no other breathing equipment, he would just have to hold his breath. On a quick impulse he fumbled out his sunglasses and put them on, hoping they might save his eyes from the worst of the ash. Then, with a deep breath, he turned the plane.

The dive was less than perfect, and his panicked scramble out of the smoke had left him higher than usual, but he hit the spray regardless and the familiar white trail formed behind the aircraft. He turned the spray off and turned for another pass. Beneath him on the ground he could see people running back and forth to a pipe in the yard with buckets, damping down the surfaces of the house. Charred marks in the grass showed where smaller fires had already been dowsed as they had ignited, perhaps sparked by the heat and ash in the air. This time the pass was near perfect, despite his watering eyes, and the spray he left behind him swept the yard and the house. He turned again, wanting to make sure the house was thoroughly covered, taking deep breaths in the clearer air away from the fire. On the ground it must be a nightmare.

The tank was mostly full when he began his flight, and he emptied it. By the time he was finished the house, cars, and yard were soaking, and the bare earth of the makeshift firebreak shone a muddy brown. Where smouldering ash touched the glistening surface it fizzled and went out.

He peeled away to return home, the long flight giving him time to take a quiet pride in a job well done. First, he reminded himself, there was something else to do.

"C-SPRY 10 returning to Brooke's Vale. I've saturated the house, smoke was too thick to get to the fire." He sent his second transmission on the emergency channel a little warily.

"Acknowledged. Congratulations on your first mission." The tone was flat and professional, but the words were not. Matt was still grinning to himself forty minutes later when he touched down.

At the airfield the others had not been idle. As soon as they watched him take off, Jake had headed into town, returning a few minutes later with his mobile water tender. He backed it carefully into place by the well.

"Come on. If we can get the water tender hooked up and filled it'll make refilling the spray tank a lot quicker." Jake looked round for help. "Where's Jim?"

"He said he had someone to speak to. Don't worry, I've got the time. It's not like I need to go home." Rose grinned, picked up her tools and walked across to the tender. The well pump, slower but all-electric would fill it, and then once the plane arrived back the powerful diesel engine in the tender could transfer the water to the plane much more quickly.

"What about your Gran? Doesn't she want company?" Jake asked, and Rose laughed.

"She was out of here before the power went down. She likes her creature comforts, does Gran."

"She must like having you around then, at her beck and call," Jake teased, holding the pipe steady as Rose twisted the spanner on the joint.

"Yes and no." Rose virtually growled, as she put both hands on the wrench and yanked it round another turn.

"Oh?"

"She thinks I need to get –

" – Some nice dresses and make-up –

" – And stop doing all these rough things," Rose replied, punctuating each fragment of the sentence with another twist of the spanner. She paused, ready for one last heave. "Maybe then I could find a nice young man."

The statement was said with heavy irony as she leaned over, both hands pressing on the wrench. The frustration paid dividends as the nut clicked snugly into place, the washer against it forming a tight seal. Jake looked it over, and compared it to the others on the tender.

"Not bad. But I thought you already had a nice young man?" he asked, wiping his hands on his trousers and heading for the stopcock. Rose rolled her eyes in exasperation as she put the tools away.

"You know what she's like. 'Couldn't you at least have gone for an officer?' 'What about that nice Smythe boy?' 'Have you considered a doctor, or a lawyer?' I'm enjoying a few days peace and quiet!"

"Ouch." Jake gave her a sympathetic look. "Stand back."

He turned the water on, and abruptly the hose went taut, water pouring through it and out.

"Only the leak it's meant to have," Rose said with some satisfaction, brushing her hair off her face with a greasy hand. "Better turn it off before it runs the tender dry."

"K." Jake switched it off, reached round and turned on Matt's small electrical pump. With a steady flow the tender began to fill. "Hope Matt'll forgive me for draining his battery. He gets more electricity each time the wind blows, but I'd need to go quite a way to get more diesel if we run out."

"Better to save the diesel, just in case." Rose agreed, and then frowned. "Won't you need that if there's a fire?" she asked, beginning to haul the tool bag back to the hangar. Jake offered a hand, and she passed it across gratefully.

"The tender needs to be up here to refill anyway." He shrugged. "Believe me, if a fire breaks out, I'll be having it back. By the way,

Roger wanted to know if you would kindly repair his fuse box again."

"Really?" One eyebrow lifted in pure scepticism and Jake coughed apologetically.

"No, actually he thinks you're a dangerous modern woman who might give his wife ideas. He wanted to know if I'd bring you up and 'manage' you on the job to make sure you knew your place." Jake shrugged slightly and spread his hands in a gesture of helplessness. "What can I say? It's Roger."

"Ah. Well, I know his place. And it's without electricity." Rose smiled sweetly and Jake laughed.

"Is that one of those dangerous feminist ideas?" he teased and Rose gave him an innocent look before she grinned.

"Nope. I'm just that petty."

"No manners, no power. Sounds fair," Jim chimed in, as he climbed out of his car.

"So where've I been now?" Jake asked in feigned resignation.

"You haven't. I've been up at the Sampson's place. I couldn't reach him on the phone." Jim scowled. Network outages, cables burned through and massive load as everyone tried to contact friends and family all usually

93

caused communication problems at this time of year, but knowing the causes did not make it any less inconvenient.

"What, and they let riff-raff like you through the gate? No standards anymore." Rose waved a hand dismissively in imitation of her grandmother. "Any reason in particular, or just want to see how the other half lives?"

"I wanted to make sure he wasn't going to take his microlite up. The last thing we need is to be sharing our airspace with something with no radio if Matt has to do an emergency landing."

"How did Claude take it?" Jake was a little cautious. After the fire alarm this morning, he doubted that the retired director, one of the most well-off men in Brooke's Vale, had been in a good mood.

"He took it well." Jim's tone indicated that had been a surprise to him. "He said conditions for flight weren't great, and if keeping the microlite on the ground would help fight the fire, then he wouldn't fly it. He also wanted to know if there was anything else he could do to help – even offered us his grass field for landing."

"Ok." Jake laughed in relief. "After the Barnehursts that's nice to hear."

"He said it was the least he could do after all your work this morning. We can't use his field, it's too short, but the thought was there." As Jim finished, Jake nodded in appreciation. The fire marshal's job was often thankless and it was nice to have someone acknowledge it. Quick sharp steps echoed on the concrete and Jill peered in.

"I thought I'd see how you were doing," she said, seeing the group.

"Should you be leaving the radio unmanned?" Jim asked and Jill opened her bag. Inside the three mobiles were neatly tucked in and activated.

"Now that Matt's up, they're co-ordinating with him directly. All I can do is listen in, since he only has a scanner in the office. They already know to reach me on mobile if there's an emergency." She looked a little frustrated.

"You should have volunteered as a pilot," Rose teased, and the older woman laughed.

"So I can listen to them politely refuse? They've got a crop sprayer pilot and a military pilot available with thousands of hours flight time. I don't think a retired widow with a private pilot's licence and a couple of hundred hours is really in the same league. So, how's the water doing?" They all looked up towards the little water tender, still steadily filling.

"Pretty good," Jake said. "We've got my tender, the mains, and Matt's well and electric pump. I'm not so worried we'll run out of water, it's just the time it takes to fill it up."

"With all that water I'm surprised you didn't suggest spraying the valley down," Jim said. Now that they had a call sign and something to do to help, he was less worried about giving Jake alternatives.

"Half of it's salt. Want to tell me what happens if you spray large amounts of concentrated salt water on plants?" Jake raised an eyebrow, and Jim shook his head. Jill tutted.

"You'd kill half the plants in the valley and raise an awful stink. I suppose it doesn't matter as much near the fire since the plants are dead anyway?" she said, and Jake nodded.

"Exactly. And if the fire never came here, you'd have caused all that damage for nothing."

"Insurance wouldn't cover that, would it?" Jill asked rhetorically, and Jake shook his head.

"Nope, but the pilots could get sued." Unspoken in all their minds was the name Barnehurst, a man who would take great pleasure in suing the airstrip.

"OK, OK, I get the point." Jim held his hands up in mock surrender. "Shouldn't you check on your water tender?"

Another quick round of checks and alternative ways to fill the water tank were investigated, but they all knew they were filling time until the aircraft returned. Shortly before Matt was due back Jill disappeared into the house, and a moment later stuck a hand out of the door, thumb raised. The others took positions by the fuel and water hoses, looking across the sky to see if they could spot the yellow dot of the crop sprayer returning. Jim saw it first, experience as a pilot telling. He knew the angle it would approach at and what he was looking for, and pointed it out. As the sun reflected off the wings, Rose and Jake caught sight of it. Faintly the engine could be heard and then the dot took on shape and form, its edges hard to make out in the bright sky. A few minutes later and the crop sprayer landed and taxied to its bay. Waiting until the propeller stopped, they ran across, ignoring Matt as he opened the cockpit, and began to fix the hoses.

The water refuelling procedure was not perfect, but it was beginning to gel. With a long hose attached to the water tender's intake and trailed down the well, the water tender could pump water into the aircraft's tank almost as fast as it took it in. Although used in that fashion it ate diesel, it managed the bulk of the work, leaving them to top the tank off while the tender was refilled by the small electric pump by the well.

An hour later and Matt was back up in the air on his next mission. Another farmstead was threatened, this one near to Pine Lees, north west of Lydford. In this situation the homestead was threatened by one of the main fire fronts, and there was no question of taking on the fire directly with the crop sprayer. Instead Matt's instructions were to damp down as much of the farm as he could to try to assist the occupants in saving their home.

The easy way to find Pine Lees was usually to fly to the Forest Gorge, turn and follow its length to the road bridge and along. The main road and gorge made a very visible landmark for pilots, and Matt knew it intimately. This time however, he knew he needed to move quickly. With his paper map to one side, he was also watching the GPS screen, looking for a closer landmark. Taking a chance he turned, cutting in what should be a straight line towards the house. As he did, he saw the fire front. It was miles away yet, but down towards the road bridge, the fire was pushing forward. There did not seem to be any crews down there, but then the gorge itself was a massive natural firebreak, so they had probably decided to let it burn itself out. He pulled his eyes away from the fire, and began to scan the ground ahead, looking for the house. Described as a large white building with a slate roof, in cleared land surrounded by forest, it should be easy to find. As he saw the main road ahead, he looked along it and then turned slightly north. His fascination with the fire front had pulled him slightly off-course.

As he turned he saw his target, and allowed himself a triumphant grin. He had not been that far out after all, and had managed to shave minutes off the journey. Quickly he announced his location over radio and then began a first low pass to judge the conditions. As he swung passed he frowned. Something was not right.

"C-SPRY 10 to Base. The house is empty and closed up." Matt circled, puzzled. He could understand spraying the house anyway, but the original details had been quite firm that a family would be here. A low pass confirmed that all the windows were closed, the garage shut and locked and there was no sign of any cars. He circled again trying to decide what to do.

"C-SPRY 10 Received. Await new instructions." Matt was barely listening. A sudden realisation hit him and he turned the crop sprayer, flying along the road out. If the family had been here when he was instructed and had only just left then they would not have had time to go far. A couple of minutes flight up the road produced no results, and he turned back, flying straight to the house. The other way the road led to the gorge and road bridge, a natural firebreak, but the fire was closing on it fast. He followed the road back, silently praying he would not find them, only to see a small family car heading down the forest road towards the gorge.

It was twenty-three miles of road to the bridge, and they would cover it in just under half an hour. The fire was burning only a few miles from the road, and spreading fast. Unless they speeded up, it would cut them off. Matt hit transmit.

"C-SPRY 10 to base. There's a car on the road to Forest Gorge road bridge."

"C-SPRY 10 confirm location?" Matt looked quickly at the map, then realised the squares covered a lot of area and fell back on local knowledge.

"C-SPRY 10 to base. They're coming down from Pine Lees towards the Road Bridge, about twenty miles from the Bridge."

"C-SPRY 10 can you contact them?"

"No. The trees are too close for a low pass."

"C-SPRY 10, we're diverting a rescue crew, can you keep the car in sight?"

"Yes, err, C-SPRY 10 to Base. Yes." Matt found himself distracted as the car continued to head further towards the danger zone. The fire front was only a few scant miles from the road. If they could get across the road bridge, they would be safe, but with smoke and ash on the road the conditions were hindering them

101

dangerously. Unless the fire was slowed, they would be cut off.

Matt pulled the crop sprayer away from the car, turning towards the fire. For a moment he wished he had remembered to bring a scarf as the smoke began to sting his eyes, and then he was too busy thinking of angles and approaches to care. He did not dare use the water dump; if he missed and hit the car even indirectly the force of water could knock the vehicle off the road. He aimed his run to be parallel along the fire front, hit the spray and then forgot about it, as he focused on keeping the crop sprayer straight and level. Snatching quick shallow breaths, the hot air stung his throat, and his mouth tasted of ash. Finally, mercifully the pass was complete and he pulled the crop sprayer into a climb, turning the spray off and blinking to clear his tearing eyes.

His spray had kicked up a cloud of steam and smoke above the trees, and the car driver had obviously seen the danger. The car accelerated, trying to get to the road bridge before the fire could reach the road. It would be touch and go, but Matt could not simply watch.

This close to the fire the turbulence was a problem, and the crop sprayer was difficult to control. He struggled with it, trying to bring the aircraft round and lined up for a run low enough that the spray could have an effect. Relying as much on the feel of the aircraft as his instruments, Matt took a deep breath and then dived in a shallow run above the trees ahead of the fire front. The cabin filled with smoke, and he held the run straight for a few seconds, before realising the view would not clear. Quickly he curtailed the run, killing the spray as he lifted away from the trees.

The driver's frantic speed was eating the miles between the car and the road bridge. Only fifteen miles remained to the bridge, and safety. The fire was closer now and a smoky haze was drifting across the road and wafting into the sky, obscuring vision and clogging in throats. The strip between the road and the fire front was becoming ever narrower. Rather than take the time to turn back, Matt pulled a tight turn and performed his run down the line he had just completed, spray on.

As he passed the car he swung into another tight turn over the fire, still spraying, trying to keep the fire clear of the road just long enough. From the cockpit the road bridge was now in sight, but ahead of them the fire was almost by the roadside. Swinging back again, as he circled between the fire and the car, he rubbed a wrist across his forehead to get rid of the sweat. His hand came away black from soot.

Hitting the spray he began his next run back towards the car, struggling against the winds that tried to drive him off course. It felt as if the fire was a living thing trying to fight him, pushing the aircraft away with the jets of sparks and cinders that rose, clawing at it with ribbons of smoke. Concentrating on keeping the aircraft level and in the sky, Matt saw the disaster a moment before it happened. All he could do was shout a warning, unheard and futile in the cockpit. The driver saw it too, but turned the wheel a fraction too late to avoid the fallen branches and lost control. The car slewed sideways and stopped across the road. Its wheels spun futilely in the ditch, bonnet facing a tree. The front doors opened, and the occupants climbed out frantically.

They wrenched at the back doors, and reached inside. In the cockpit, Matt screamed at them to run. The wall of fire rushing over the hill was visible to him, but not to them. He turned the aircraft. If they could make it to the road bridge, the natural fire break of the gorge might save them. Then he saw what was taking the time, and for a moment his heart stopped. Two smaller figures, one carried, the other held by the hand, as fast as their parents could pull them. Mercifully the distance blurred detail, but the fire was almost on them.

Matt banked left, turning dangerously close to the fire. His first pass sprayed a short burst across the road behind them and he banked for another turn. If he could just buy them time… He completed his second pass without realising how close the fire had come. The cabin filled with choking ash and smoke, and he could hear the engine beginning to struggle. Cursing, tear blinded with cinder-stung eyes, he pulled the aircraft upwards and away, hoping to clear the cabin air.

The figures below him had seen the fires now, and both children were being carried. Their progress was faltering, hampered by the thick smoke that made it so difficult to breathe, and the burning winds swirling the ash around them. Matt banked for another pass, cabin clearer, but he could already see how this would end. He repeated his pattern, a series of short passes, spraying water constantly to try to stop the fire, but the spray boiled instantly as it touched the flames and he was forced away by the threat of scalding steam in the cabin.

Below him one of the figures had fallen, overcome by smoke or heat. The other turned back to help, and that was when the fire swept over them. Matt swung back desperately hitting the spray controls, but smoke and heat forced him to lift away. He could not see anything beyond the flames anymore.

The crop sprayer was limping, propeller stuttering. On reflex he hit spray, not caring particularly where it went, to dump the water and lighten the load. Then he turned for home.

Matt climbed out of the cockpit silently. The look on his face was dreadful and he ignored Jill and Rose, who were staring in shock at the aircraft's battered state. Uncertain of what to do they began to connect the fuel and water hoses to the crop sprayer, waiting for some comment that would tell them what had happened. Never demonstrative, Matt disappeared into the warehouse without a word. A few seconds later there was a loud bang, as the corrugated iron wall of the hangar shook. Rose threw a horrified glance at Jill, who was still occupied with the water hose, and rushed into the warehouse.

Matt was staring blindly at the wall, shoulders shaking silently. His outstretched arm ended in a clenched fist, embedded in a dent in the corrugated iron sheet. To her horror, blood was starting to trickle out, down towards the floor.

"Jill!" she yelled, and dived across to Matt. As his pale, stricken face turned to her, she knew that whatever he was seeing in front of him it was not the hangar around them. She turned him gently, letting him lean against the wall, allowing her to look at his hand. His back against the iron, he slid down slowly as his strength left him, hunched and still shaking. Focusing on the practical Rose turned her attention to his hand, gently coaxing it open.

"I couldn't –" he broke off, unable to find words for whatever he had to tell her.

"Hush. It's alright." Rose tried to quiet him, staring at the ruin of his hand. Matt had punched the wall full force and the skin had split open. She hoped the white objects were not broken bones within the injuries, but knew that they probably were. She waved a hand frantically behind her, beckoning to Jill who had

107

come into the hangar. The older woman handed her the first aid kit, then swallowed hard and stood up.

"I'll see if there's anyone who knows first aid available." Jill retreated rapidly, and Rose could not blame her. The injury was beyond either of their medical skills. Whatever had happened, it was not going to be easy to hear.

"Get Jim," Rose shouted after her, as a thought occurred. "He'll be taking on the flying from now on."

The next hour was a flurry of activity as Jim arrived, followed by Doctor Marcus from the far end of the valley. Rose gratefully gave up the first aid to the doctor and retreated, helping Jim set up the aircraft for another run. Knowing there was nothing he could do for Matt, Jim was going over the crop sprayer in fine detail.

Without knowing what had happened to the aircraft they could only guess at the damage it might have sustained. It was covered in soot and ash, the pitot tube partially clogged and debris caught in the hinges of the control surfaces. Leaving Rose to work on the windscreen and outer fuselage, he carefully cleaned off the control surfaces, removing blockages and adding oil, but to his surprise there seemed to be no permanent damage. The air-cooled engine was trickier, delving into the workings with a toothbrush and oil to remove the dark grey paste of ash, but he could not see any permanent problems. A little bit of fuel in the tank revealed no leaks or damage and the engine started and ran, roughly at first but then it cleared whatever obstruction was present and settled down to what Jim thought of as a comfortable mechanical chugging.

He taxied briefly on the runway and the aircraft handled correctly, all the control surfaces moving as desired and even the trim controls working adequately. Of course, there was only one way to tell if it would fly. Filling it with a little more fuel, putting a drain of water in the tank for the spray, Jim carefully took it up for a test flight on a slow circuit round Brooke's Vale.

Gingerly he tested the controls, but all the main surfaces were working. The altimeter appeared to work, so the pitot tube had probably been cleared correctly. He hit the spray and a small puff of vapour obediently appeared behind the plane. Carefully he came in to land, aware that the fixed undercarriage had been exposed to the same dangers as the rest of the aircraft. It touched down neatly, bounced as the aircraft was lighter than he remembered and then settled down. He taxied it to the refuelling bay and climbed out, shaking his head.

"Well?" Rose was hovering.

"Hook her up. I think we've been very, very, lucky." As Jim began a second look over the plane, to see if anything had become more obvious after the flight, Rose quickly hooked up the fuel and water hoses to top the tanks off after the flight. Neither of them planned to leave the crop sprayer until they were satisfied it was flyable. Whatever had happened to Matt, they did not want him to lose his aircraft as well.

As they waited, Doctor Marcus came out of the hangar deep in discussion with Jill. Looking round, he saw them and the pair walked across.

"How's Matt?" Jim cut straight to the point, and Doctor Marcus looked at him gravely.

"Shock. He's refused a sedative, so all I can suggest is keep him warm and calm."

"What about flying?" Rose asked, and the doctor looked at her in surprise.

"I wouldn't recommend it. Particularly not with that hand." His incredulous tone of voice told them more than his words.

"How badly is it broken?" Jill asked cautiously, and the doctor shook his head.

"It's not. However I had to remove paint shards and stitch the skin. Keep it cold to reduce the bruising and use it as little as possible." He looked at them. "In all seriousness, he has had an extreme shock, and will need looking after. With Rob away, you're the closest thing he's got to a family."

"Don't worry, we'll take care of him," Jill said, and the doctor nodded. Rose sighed.

"Jim, looks like you're on the flying for the foreseeable future."

"The crop sprayer is flyable?" Jill sounded surprised. Rose and Jim exchanged a glance and then both nodded.

"Yeah. We've done a test flight," Jim answered. "Most of the damage is cosmetic, but it looks like she flew through a fire. Did Matt say what happened?"

"No." Doctor Marcus was quite firm on this point. "And I would suggest not pushing him."

"Understood. Thanks Doctor." Jill nodded. The elderly doctor took the hint and nodded a gracious goodbye before he headed off.

"How is Matt?" Rose asked, once the doctor had left.

"He's not flying again today, and he won't take a painkiller, so he's on the beer." Jill's voice said a lot about her opinions of that particular option. "Anyway, how long to refill the plane?"

"About another hour. We had to give her a good going over." Jim's words were an explanation, not an apology. "You'd better let the emergency services know."

"When I saw Matt's state I told them we wouldn't be flying again. They didn't sound surprised, so they know something happened," Jill said, and then turned and began walking to the house. "I'll let them know we've got our reserve pilot ready and when we'll be able to fly. Good luck."

Jim swallowed. It was easy to volunteer to fly this, but now that he was up here nerves had hit. Even though he had checked the aircraft thoroughly, he was focusing on her handling for any tell tale signs that her ash bath had done more damage than he had thought. With dense forest below him, there was nowhere in sight to put down safely and the regular updates on the emergency channel made him uncomfortably aware of the raging fires springing up only a few miles away.

He knew how the crop sprayer flew in good conditions, and even not-so-good ones, but this was new to him and without the security of Matt's experienced voice from the back seat he was flying cautiously. Every aircraft handled slightly differently, and he still had to get used to this one, how she turned, her flying pattern and capabilities, and even any unique quirks for this particular aircraft. This one was slower than the Robin, and twice the size, but it had the cropsprayer pipes to affect handling. The large yellow panel in the middle of his controls was the water gauge, showing the level in the tank, but he found himself looking side to side often as he tried to get used to the instruments and dials.

He checked the map, telling himself to stay focused, but it was difficult. The sheer size of the smoke clouds rising ahead of him from the main fire front made them seem closer than they were, as his mind tried and failed to grasp the size of the inferno. Small black specks were visible, moving across it with purpose and adding white sprays against the black smoke. The fire-fighting aircraft, the huge Canadair and Antonov water bombers, had been turned into tiny dots by the distance as they fought their own battle against the flames. Tearing himself away from the sight, he checked the map again. Gratefully he turned west, away from the pyre burning on the horizon, and ready to play his own small part in the battle.

The gully ahead was wide, but the sides sloped. With the stream at the base near dry it would be an ineffective fire break, but the fire teams were on their way here to correct that. In the mean time, anything he could do to damp it down would help. He just had to hope he could put his two thousand litre load where it would do some good.

Jim lined up for a low pass and paused. This sort of flying was more Matt's field, low repeated passes to saturate low-lying vegetation. He admitted to himself he simply was not confidant trying it in this gully in an unfamiliar aircraft. His hand hovered above the spray and then drew back.

114

As he descended into the gully the crop sprayer's handling changed. Perhaps it was the winds, or simply that he was unfamiliar with the manoeuvre, but while she had been light on the stick in level flight on the way out, the aircraft became more difficult to control. He pulled up, checking the trim control, but even adjusting the trim did not produce a notable improvement in her handling. As he climbed away, the handling smoothed out. Great. One of this aircraft's quirks was that it apparently did not like low level flight, or at least he did not know the tricks to handle her properly at low heights.

Instead he lined up cautiously at three hundred feet above the gully floor and made his first run. Turning on the spray, he kept the aircraft level and then quickly switched it off. Cautiously he congratulated himself on a successful run, and turned the aircraft back as something caught his eye. The white cloud of spray, caught by the wind, had rolled away from the gully, soaking the trees along one top edge instead of reaching the ground. He remembered Matt saying that crop spraying was usually done at fifteen feet above ground and swore. In an unfamiliar aircraft, in an unfamiliar area, performing an unfamiliar operation, there was no way he was taking the risk. He put her into a climb, and then began to circle as he considered his problem.

As he completed a circuit, no water dropped, he snatched a careful glance at the map hoping to find an answer to his predicament. To his surprise there was. The contour lines showed quite clearly that the gully, like many, sloped and there was a place at the lower end where the stream pooled in the wet seasons. Inspired he went around again, lining up for a pass at three hundred feet on the lower end and began his second run. This time, lifting the taped-on cover Matt had added to stop the lever being used accidentally, he hit the water dump.

No fine spray was left this time. A solid mass of water shot out from below the aircraft as the spray tank dumped out its contents. The sprayer bounced in the air as the entire tank emptied in seconds. Jim had expected that, but not for the nose to pitch sharply upwards. Caught by surprise, he turned it into a shallow ascent, uncertain if the aircraft would pitch downwards again the moment the tank was empty. Grip tight on the stick, grateful his target area was so large, he held the aircraft steady, running along the line of the gully until the tank gauge showed it had finished a moment later, and then climbed away. As he looked back the gully was awash, water running down the banks and into the stream, which looked like a torrent. He grinned to himself, and then the grin quickly faded.

Below him, the water at the edges of the stream was beginning to soak into the parched earth, drying and evaporating in the hot sun. He turned for home, hoping he had at least achieved something.

"Two hours to fill that tank. Two minutes to empty it." Jake commented in disgust, leaning on the side of the water tender, as Jim looked the crop sprayer over. Rose and Jill had quickly connected the hoses for fuel and water in a routine that was becoming practiced.

"More like ten seconds actually." Jim said, deliberately provoking his brother. Jake refused to take the bait, launching a barb of his own.

"Well at least we know it got somewhere useful. My little brother doing something right. Who'd have thought it?" Jake had always been better at pushing Jim's buttons, and he knew exactly which issue to raise.

"Little brother? Fourteen minutes. Fourteen minutes thirty years ago and I have to put up with this for the rest of my life!" Jim turned to appeal to Rose, who shook her head at him.

"Nothing to do with me. I'm just filling your water tank. I'm not getting involved in your domestic disputes."

"Fine, then you didn't hear this either. Jim, thanks for taking on the Dromader. We thought we'd be a plane down after what happened." Jake chuckled slightly. "Apparently you have no idea the stir Jill caused when she phoned in and said that C-SPRY 10 was going to keep flying. Until it became clear you'd changed pilots, they were trying to find a way to politely refuse on the grounds he'd done more than enough." He shrugged and then realised the others were watching him carefully.

"Matt hasn't said anything since he came back." Rose said slowly. "He walked into the hangar and punched the wall. He's been on the beer ever since." Jake's eyes widened slightly and he looked at the others. Jim and Jill both nodded their agreement, and he swallowed and gestured them closer, lowering his voice in case it could somehow carry to the lone figure sitting by the hangar.

"A family died in front of him. The rescue team saw it all. They picked up Matt's transmission and were coming across the road bridge at the time."

"Christ. What happened?" Rose blinked and looked away, ashamed of herself for asking.

"The fire overtook them. I don't have all the details but apparently Matt tried to keep it off them with the crop sprayer. The crew chief said it was an insane bit of flying."

"Is there any chance –?" She broke off, already knowing the answer.

"None. The heat was too intense for the fire crew to get through. They were just at the wrong place at the wrong time." Jake stopped to let the others think it through. He refrained from adding that it was the victims' own fault for leaving it far too late to leave, and failing to respond to the evacuation signal they had been given.

"Hard lines," Jim said, with a quick look across at Matt. "Was there anything he could have done?"

"In a Dromader, against an established blaze that size? Not a hope. For what it's worth, the crew chief was quite impressed. He said Matt held it together long enough to dump the remaining water on the fire. It bought the crew time to get back across the bridge, or they'd have been fighting the whole way."

"I don't think that's what Matt was thinking when he dumped the tank." Jim replied dryly.

"Then don't say anything. Right now people are losing homes, pets, families and friends. If a mistake over his motives acts as a morale boost, it's what the crews need."

"Is that why I got the gully duty?"

"Yeah. They know you aren't in a familiar aircraft, so you get the easy jobs to break you in." Jake grinned. "If you've got time before dark, you'll be back at the gully dumping another load. They're setting it up as a major firebreak."

"Depends on the refill. We need a good pressurised water source." Jim shrugged. "Without it, we can't really speed things up. Your tender's got a decent pump on it, but it holds less than a quarter of the tank. Once that's empty we're stuck with the well, Matt's water tank and the mains, and things get slow. We're having to refill the tender from the well during flights, but there's a limit to how much you can draw from that at once."

"It's what I was concerned about." Jake admitted. "If you simply couldn't refill with water fast enough to be useful. But right now, they're just throwing numbers at it. If they can get enough planes airborne it doesn't matter how long each individual one takes."

"Then how long to sunset?" Jim asked, suddenly all business.

"Hour and twenty." Jill replied and Jim looked at the map again.

"If we fill the tank to three quarters – that's fifteen hundred litres – I'll still have time to get there and back before dark with a bit of leeway. Ask them if that's what they want to do." Jim's tone was not a suggestion, it was a command, and Jill nodded and vanished inside. "Jake, can you tell me if you know of any fires on this route?" He traced it with his finger, virtually a straight line from Brooke's Vale to the gully. Jake shook his head.

"Fuel's full." Rose said, as she disconnected the hose. Jim nodded.

"Thanks. Can you stand away from the aircraft? I'd like to give her a walk round." The water hose was still connected, but Jim ignored it, checking control surfaces and tires. Once he was satisfied he went on to the full walk round on Matt's list. By the hangar, the other pilot had stirred and was watching the proceedings with faint interest, but Jim ignored him until he had finished.

"You are good to go." Jill had walked back, but let him finish his checks before she interrupted. "Same gully, same procedure, as much water as possible."

"Fine." Jim nodded.

Quickly Rose disconnected the water hose, under the pilot's watchful eye, and then the others stood clear. Jim settled himself in the cockpit, looking at the huge water gauge that showed the tank currently held just over sixteen hundred litres, and forced himself to relax. Then he started the engines.

The take-off was surprisingly quick. He did not want to waste time and simply gained as much speed as he could before he lowered the nose. As he felt the tail come up, the aircraft lifted off almost immediately. Angling the sprayer into a shallow climb to clear the rise at the valley entrance, he hoped to gain some extra airspeed before he settled into level flight. On paper he had plenty of time, but he wanted to make sure he had some leeway. It was twenty minutes there and back at the crop sprayer's maximum speed, but that left half an hour for take off, landing, operations, turbulence and anything else that could go wrong. After the beating the aircraft had taken earlier he was concerned about the effect of running the engine at full power for the entire journey. He climbed to two thousand feet, hoping that the conditions would be smooth for the flight, and increased airspeed. Flying directly into a headwind, Jim adjusted his arrival estimates accordingly and sucked his breath through his teeth. Five extra minutes flying. Hopefully, with the wind behind him, he would make it up on the way back.

Nervously, he adjusted the trim, trying to ensure the aircraft's handling was in good shape. He knew that the crop sprayer was surprisingly light to fly in stable conditions but it had a reputation for being heavy and occasionally unstable in winds or close to hillsides. He wanted everything set up just right for the pass, and still had no idea how close the fire was to the gully now.

"C-SPRY 10 to Base. What is the situation at the target location?"

"Base to C-SPRY 10. Crews are clear of the gully. What is your time of arrival?"

"C-SPRY 10 to Base. Eight minutes."

"Base to C-SPRY 10. Understood and relayed."

Jim didn't respond, looking ahead to the gully. On one side of the valley the trees had been felled along the hillside. As he approached, pulling wide to get into position for the run, he could faintly see the fire crews working among them. The fire lines were visible in the distance beyond them, but the smoke in the cabin was no worse than on the ground. He turned on the crop sprayer's lights anyway, hoping to make sure he could be seen.

"C-SPRY 10, ready to water drop on target." There was a pause before the response came.

"C-SPRY 10, crews confirm they are clear. Proceed."

He slowed the crop sprayer, losing as much speed as he could before he began the run. He would gain speed naturally on the dive through the gully, and wanted to give himself as much time as he could for the tank to empty.

This pass would have to be lower than his first, to limit the amount of water splashed away from the target.

He turned the aircraft downward into a shallow dive to try to reduce her acceleration, waited until he could see the crop sprayer was over the gully, and pulled the emergency dump. Once again a solid mass of water shot from below the aircraft, and it jolted as the load lightened. The crop sprayer yawed, and Jim corrected hastily as she rocked. He was lower than he had planned, entirely his mistake, and this close to the ground the aircraft was reacting badly in the winds that blew through the gully. Grimly he concentrated on holding her level, wishing he had more experience with this type of flying, and then the water gauge showed empty. Immediately he climbed away, grateful that the drop was over. Once he had pulled the crop sprayer back to level flight, he thumbed the radio.

"C-SPRY 10 to Base. Drop Complete. Returning to Brooke's Vale"

"Base to C-SPRY 10. Ground crews confirmed successful drop."

Jim looked below and to his left as a flurry of motion drew his attention. In the midst of the forest an orange spark caught his eye, and then as he watched it caught hold. With terrifying speed the hillside ignited, a mile long stretch of trees going up in moments. Despite knowing that the sooner he was back at the airstrip the sooner he could refill it was hard to tear himself away.

Beyond the fire, he realised the trees had been pulled down to create a firebreak. Even knowing that the trees had been felled and that the crews were standing by, Jim's mouth went dry as he watched. It seemed impossible they could keep it under control. The vision of a fire like this at Brooke's Vale was the stuff nightmares were made of.

With the water tank empty there was nothing he could do if it did get out of control. He pulled away from the area, getting clear in case any of the fire fighting aircraft were on their way. Although the fire was still raging, it seemed to have stopped spreading. An occasional water jet raised by one of the edges, but in the main the fire crews seemed content to let it burn itself out. Once the controlled blaze had disposed of all the fuel, there would be nothing for the main fire front to exploit once it reached here.

126

The new firebreak would be less than forty miles from Brooke's Vale, even if it was to the southeast and not in a direct line. Suddenly chilled, Jim turned for home.

Night fell as he returned. Too tired to talk, the small group secured the plane and crawled into Matt's house. Rose and Jill were asleep quickly in the spare rooms, but Jim found it harder to relax. As the adrenaline of the day's flights wore off, he became aware of a persistent nagging ache in his legs and back. Every time he closed his eyes he saw the fire springing up again, and when he actually fell asleep visions of the valley burning awaited him. Finally he gave up and walked outside for some air. The reassuring smell of engine oil and grease from the planes almost covered the wood smoke on the wind, but right now he just wanted somewhere quiet to think. Quietly he retrieved his car keys and left the airfield.

Jim drove up the hill, and stopped his car. The little lay-by by the valley entrance on top of the hill was a good lookout point and, as he climbed out of the car and stretched, he paused. In the dusk the smoke was no longer visible, but the fires marked orange lines clearly in the darkness. Around them he knew the fire fighters would still be out there, working to extinguish and contain the blazes. Slowly he scanned the horizon, suppressing a curse as he realised that the fires could be seen slowly, remorselessly, moving. To have movement discernable at this distance, the fires themselves must be moving incredibly quickly.

There was a thump from behind him, and he jumped and turned.

"Dammit Matt, don't do that."

"Beer?" The sardonic comment was utterly unapologetic, as the older pilot held up a can he had pulled free from a six pack. Jim sat down on the log next to him and took it gratefully.

"Ring pulls? How old are these?"

"Beer never goes off. If you don't want it…" Matt reached for the can, but Jim evaded him.

"Never said that, did I?" Jim took a deep swallow, scanning the horizon again in disbelief. "Never seen anything like it."

"Nor I." Matt took a swallow of his own, a shadow of pain on his face. "They're losing out there."

"What's the latest?"

"I turned off the radio an hour ago. They'd just lost Lydford. Fires have spread a bit since then." Matt gestured vaguely at the horizon, ignoring Jim's shock at the news the little town was gone.

"Is there anything we can do?" The question was desperate, rhetorical and born of the frantic need to do something, anything, rather than sit here and let the fire happen. Matt shook his head.

"She's not rigged for night flight. We'd just be in the way." There was a long pause and then Matt sighed.

"Best you hear it from me. Lucy didn't make it. They found the car."

"Fuck." It was the only thing he could think to say. The matronly shopkeeper had been a fixture of Jim's life as long as he could remember. A thousand questions were running through his mind, but he was too afraid of the answers to ask them. Matt stared at his beer can.

"For what it's worth she didn't suffer. They found her curled up in the back seat. The smoke got her in her sleep. She just never woke up."

"That fucking junker must have broken down again." Jim tried to tell himself that he was not crying, that his eyes only stung from the smoke, as he tried to shake the image of the old shopkeeper settling herself into the back seat of her broken down car. He broke, dropping his head into his hands. Matt allowed the time to pass in silence, watching the orange flames on the horizon, and finished his beer.

"Sunrise is at 5:18 tomorrow," he advised, opening another can. Jim raised his head. If he had been crying there was no sign.

"I'll be ready at five."

Day Two

As he had promised, Jim was ready and waiting in the cockpit as five struck. The others had been up and working earlier, and the little crop sprayer was fully loaded and fuelled. Jill had signed in on the radio and got his mission details and route prepared for the morning. Pre-flight checks complete, sitting on the runway with the engine running, all Jim needed now was light.

Finally, painfully slowly, the sky lightened and he flipped to the emergency channel and waited for a pause on the already-busy frequency. He could hear other aircraft from bases further east, airborne and on their way to fight the fire.

"C-SPRY 10, taking off from Brooke's Vale for assigned target." Announcing his intentions, he began his take-off run. This was the danger point, where burgeoning familiarity could lead a pilot to be overconfident, and overconfidence can kill quickly in an aircraft. Nonetheless, the crop sprayer was handling well and after a smooth take-off he climbed to two thousand feet and turned south towards the fires and his first job of the morning.

His target was a field on the other side of the main road between Lydford and Lowry, the nearest village to Brooke's Vale. The fire had not reached far beyond Lydford yet, but when it did the road's four lanes would make a natural fire break. In these arid conditions, if the winds picked up and carried debris and ash across it, the dry fields on the other side would go up almost instantly so the fire crews and air support had been dispatched to turn it into a more effective defence. Remembering his first dreadful attempt at spraying the gully down he fervently hoped he had learned enough to avoid disgracing himself this time. If Lowry was under threat, it brought the fire uncomfortably close to home.

Although Jim knew he would not be comfortable at Matt's quoted fifteen feet, he decided that under a hundred was both possible and manageable. In theory, if he knew the wind direction and speed it should be easy enough to work out where to drop the spray so it would be on target. In practice he suspected it would probably be trial and error. He would just have to hope he got enough of his payload on the area to soak it.

"Base to C-SPRY 10, Please confirm you are trained in low-level or formation flight?" The voice from the radio signalling him directly caught his attention, and he replied quickly.

"C-SPRY 10 to Base. Extensive experience."

"Base to C-SPRY 10. What is your flying experience?"

"C-SPRY 10 to Base. Military transport pilot. Formerly maritime patrol and early warning."

"Base to C-SPRY 10. Changing assigned target. Proceed to Forest Gorge by Pine Lees. Maintain altitude one thousand feet." Jim blinked, privately grateful that Matt had not received that signal. He turned to the new course, confirming his bearing and signalled again.

"C-SPRY 10 to Base. What is the situation?"

"Base to C-SPRY 10. Canyon floor fire. Switch your radio to the local channel and listen for F-147. She's the lead on this one."

"C-SPRY 10 to Base. Understood." Curious, Jim did as directed, checking Matt's list of frequencies and changing his radio channel in time to catch the end of another transmission.

"- to F-147. On our way to Pine Lees. Arriving in three minutes."

"F-147 to C-SPRY 3. Acknowledged." As the pilot answered, Jim transmitted his own message.

"C-SPRY 10 to F-147. ETA Pine Lees in five minutes."

"F-147 to C-SPRY 10. Acknowledged." There was a pause and then the transmission continued. "F-147 to all. The fire's jumped the gorge at Pine Lees and the floor of the gorge is on fire. The crews can't get to it quickly, so we need to get it under control." Jim whistled to himself. With the gorge floor on fire, the wind could carry burning ash out, restarting fires at the top of the cliffs even as they were extinguished. If vegetation on the cliff walls had caught, this flight would be a nightmare.

"C-SPRY 3 to F-147. What are flight conditions?"

"F-147 to all. Poor. Visibility is low and wind shear in the gorge will be a problem." Jim cringed as he heard that. He already knew the crop sprayer did not like turbulence. The voice continued. "We will form two groups. C-SPRY 6, 10 and 12 you have water loads. On my signal, dump them in quick succession by the upstream section. F-204, F-147 and C-SPRY 3 with chemical retardants will then drop downstream to make a firebreak. Any issues?"

"C-SPRY 6 to F-147. Visibility is too poor. Sorry, this is beyond me." Jim could hear the frustration in the other pilot's voice at being forced to withdraw. It was the only sensible thing to do, but the pilot obviously was not happy about it.

"F-147 to C-SPRY 6. Understood. Turn south at two thousand feet and request a new target from base."

"C-SPRY 6 to F-147. Thanks. Good luck. Over."

As the transmission paused, Jim thought it over carefully. He had extensive experience of low flying in transport planes, but he did not know the crop sprayer that well. The equipment that assisted in the large military aircraft were missing, and he would have to do this purely on his own judgement and basic instruments. Reluctantly he decided it should be possible, hoping fervently he was not overestimating his skill as a pilot.

The gorge was wide, carved by the stream that ran through the floor of the canyon. Although the streambed was dry in summer if they dumped the water upstream then, even if the aircraft missed, the lay of the land would carry it into the fire. Jim supposed the theory made sense, but right now he was mainly concerned with finding the other aircraft that would form his group. They were at five hundred feet separation, which should be just visible to each other.

"F-204 to F-147. I'm over the canyon, but visibility is close to zero. The smoke's too thick to descend."

"F-147 to F-204, get clear and hold position at five hundred feet. We need to time the drops as close together as possible to have best effect." Jim took a sharp breath, not really listening to the conversation. Ahead of him the gorge had come into view, but the edges of the cliff were obscured by the thick black clouds of smoke rising from within it. On one side the fire was solidly ablaze, throwing smoke and ash into the air. On the other the browns and faded greens of a desiccated pine forest were marked by harsh black scars and orange flames, where the fire had jumped the gorge; spread by burning embers and hot ash carried by the wind.

"Isn't there anything bigger available?" The plaintive voice from the radio said exactly what Jim was thinking, although the sharp profanity afterwards probably meant that the pilot had not meant to transmit it.

"F-147 to all. No, just us. The winds prevent loads dropped above the gorge from reaching the fire. We have to go into the gorge to ensure the drops reach their target. The winds are strong enough to carry burning material from the gorge floor out over the top of the canyon, so until it's out the ground crews are in a holding action." Around the smoke clouds, Jim caught sight of another aircraft. He hit transmit.

"C-SPRY 10 to F-147 I can see a red helicopter. I'm at a thousand feet and south side of the gorge." As he watched the helicopter pivoted neatly in place.

"F-204 to C-SPRY 10, that's me. You're the yellow fixed wing?"

"C-SPRY 10 to F-204. Confirmed." For good measure he waggled the wings briefly.

"C-SPRY 12 to C-SPRY 10. I have visual on you both. C-SPRY 10, stay on your current course and slow to one hundred mph. I'm coming down to join you from three thousand feet." Looking at the airspeed indicator, Jim did a hasty conversion to kilometres as he slowed. The Polish aircraft he was flying did everything in metric, and it was a weird adjustment.

Looking up curiously, his first glimpse of the other aircraft was a spot of reflected sunlight as it turned, descending and then it was behind him and he lost sight of it. A moment later it had pulled up ahead and to the right, keeping a good separation between them.

In the smoke, he could not immediately identify it. The biplane was almost the same size as his crop sprayer, but its wide fuselage was less streamlined. Painted white from nose to tail, it was covered in soot, obscuring its identity markings. He had an impression of enormous wing flaps, and behind them the characteristic pipes of a crop sprayer were clearly visible.

"C-SPRY 10 to C-SPRY 12. I have visual."

"C-SPRY 3 to F-204, I have visual on you." The new voice cut in suddenly.

"F-204 to C-SPRY 3, Visual confirmed. Hold altitude and stay on the north side of the gorge. I'll stay stationary."

"F-147 to C-SPRY 10 and 12. All other aircraft are on the other side of the canyon and clear of your airspace. Ready to go?"

"C-SPRY 12. Yes Ma'am."

"C-SPRY 10. Ready."

"C-SPRY 12 to 10. Suggest I go first. I can go slower, and might get some of that smoke out of the way." The tone was faintly amused, and very, very, confident. Hoping the other pilot's confidence was not misplaced, Jim responded.

"C-SPRY 10 to 12. Go ahead."

The white biplane pealed away, slowing as it turned and spiralled down into the gorge at its widest point. It was moving well below the stall speed for Jim's crop sprayer, almost floating into the smoke, and he could see why the other pilot would volunteer to go first. To his surprise, the white biplane dropped out of sight below the cliff, and his breath caught. Even with its eerily floating flight, the pilot was taking a dreadful chance in those conditions. A moment later and a cloud of white vapour became visible above the gorge edge, and then the biplane climbed slowly out of the gorge and lifted away.

"C-SPRY 12 to C-SPRY 10. Be careful of turbulence, it's worst below three hundred feet."

"C-SPRY 10 to C-SPRY 12. Thanks for the heads up." Jim replied, planning his own pass. He was not intending to drop below the cliff top anyway. Flying into the gorge in that smoke was not a good idea.

"C-SPRY 12 to F-147. Returning the Lakeside to refill." Without further discussion the biplane turned south, away from the fire but into the strong headwind, and began to accelerate. It topped out somewhere just over a hundred, even as F-147 confirmed they had received the transmission. No matter how good it might be at manoeuvring, it definitely was not a speedster.

Jim looked across the gorge, where the steam was clearing. Fortunately the wind was carrying it towards the fire. He could not emulate the other aircraft's low speed precision, and mentally mapped out a drop slightly further upstream, taking advantage of the local geography to carry the water into the blaze. He would have to use the dump and hope that the water did not evaporate.

"C-SPRY 10 to F-147. Ready to begin run." He wiped the sweat from his forehead, telling himself it was due to the heat of the forest fire and not nerves. The other pilot had made it look easy, but the crop sprayer was not as manoeuvrable as the biplane and required greater speed. The light smoke in this part of the canyon still impaired visibility, and he had found out the hard way that this aircraft did not like variable winds.

He turned in a wider circle and lined the plane up for a straight run down the gorge, planning to dip briefly between the walls much as he had with the gully. It would be a faster, higher pass than the biplane's, but there was a straight half-mile stretch before the gorge turned so he should have plenty of space. He lined up in a shallow descent over the trees, and then as the edge of the cliff passed under him he pointed the crop sprayer down into the gorge. Almost instantly he hit dump, feeling the familiar jolt, and then the aircraft shook as unpredictable winds seized it and tried to toss it into the canyon walls. He increased power, trying to hold her straight and climb out, and then suddenly he lost lift. For a sickening moment the aircraft plummeted, the straps cutting into his shoulders all that held him in the seat. Then he was past it, over two hundred feet lower into the canyon than he wanted, with a cabin full of smoke. Half-blind he pushed the aircraft into a steep climb, trusting the instruments that said he had not changed direction and praying he would not hit the canyon wall. He did not care whether the tank had emptied or not, he was getting out of this. Some risks were too great.

Then there was only sky above him, and he realised suddenly that he was clear. As he took a shuddering breath he was stunned to realise the whole thing had taken only seconds. The water tank gauge ran empty as he watched.

"F-147 to C-SPRY 10 Confirm?" There was genuine worry in the other pilot's tone, and he realised he had come out behind the smoke plume.

"C-SPRY 10 to F-147. I hit an air pocket. Small one. No damage to the aircraft. Tank's empty. Returning to Brooke's Vale, at fifteen hundred feet." He hoped his voice did not sound as shaken as he felt, but had to admit it was likely. The last time he had hit an air pocket he had dropped a thousand feet, but at thirty thousand he had had it to spare. This time the options had been more limited.

"F-147 to C-SPRY 10. Acknowledged and thanks. F-147 to F-204. Ready?"

"F-104 to F-147. I can't drop south side. The wind's too strong for the bucket."

"F-147 to F-204. Relocate to the C-SPRYs' drop location."

"F-204 to F-147. Commencing drop." To get back to Brooke's Vale, Jim had to turn north, but the area of the fire lay directly between him and his base. Not wanting to risk a collision, he climbed to fifteen hundred feet and turned a wide curve around the area.

"F-147 to F-204. Acknowledged." As he looped round, Jim got a good view of the operation he had been part of. It might have been wishful thinking, but the smoke billowing from the chasm appeared to have lessened slightly. The helicopter was hovering above the gorge, carefully lowering its suspended water bucket where C-SPRY 10 and 12 had dropped

145

their cargos. With consummate skill the pilot was inching the helicopter down the gorge, trying to get the bucket as close to their target as possible.

With a sudden shock the helicopter appeared to jump up in the air. Then it lifted almost vertically, the collapsed bucket being winched up rapidly beneath it.

"F-204. Drop completed." The smoke was no longer rising from that part of the gorge. Instead white clouds appeared to have coated the bottom. His turn complete, Jim set course for Brooke's Vale, reluctantly losing sight of the aircraft behind him. The voices from the radio continued.

"F-204 to F-147. We're clear. Going to the lake to refill. Back in ten minutes."

"F-147 to F-204 Acknowledged. C-SPRY 3, you are clear to begin your run."

"C-SPRY 3 on approach ma'am." Jim shook his head, slightly amazed. With the mix of backgrounds, pilots, aircraft and protocols this should have been a nightmare. Instead the fire fighter in F-147 had managed to keep them together as a team.

"C-SPRY 3 dump complete. Heading to River's Green to refill." Jim frowned. He did not know River's Green and had to assume it was another airstrip like Brooke's Vale, pressed into service in the emergency. Either that or someone had given an operations name to an existing airport.

"F-147 to C-SPRY 3. Thanks. Are you clear?"

"C-SPRY 3 is clear, ma'am."

"F-147 beginning run." There was a pause and then "F-147 to base. Drop complete. Fire seems to be contained."

"Base to F-147. Good job. Ground crews on site in twenty minutes, continue to act as spotter until then."

"F-147 to base. Acknowledged." Then there was silence from the radio. Jim flew on, Brooke's Vale finally in sight, and turned the radio back to the general emergency channel. Between F-147 watching the area, and the helicopter F-204 delivering its regular payload of water and foam, he was confident that this fire at least was under control.

After the exhausting operation and an uneventful return flight, Jim landed back at Brooke's Vale, taxiing to the bay almost automatically. To his relief, Matt was standing

147

by the water tank waiting for him. The crop sprayer pilot's damaged hand was encased in a tight black glove, probably to reduce swelling and stop the bandages getting dirty, but at least he was up and moving. Jill and Rose were standing by with the fuel and water hoses, and as he stopped the aircraft they were connecting them almost as he climbed out. Now that he was on firm ground, he was beginning to get over the scare in the canyon, but he knew it had still been a very near thing.

"Jim, can you phone your base?" Rose looked tired, but not especially concerned.

"Why? What's up?"

"They phoned your mobile to ask you to report in. I said you were unavailable because you were flying C-SPRY 10 for the emergency services and they asked you to call in as soon as you got back." She waited expectantly. Jim refrained from correcting her, although he had been in the military long enough to know that 'asked' was a euphemism, and headed indoors. If it was something important, there would be hell to pay if they could not reach him. After the flight he had had, all that was needed was for him to slip and swear at an officer, and that would round the morning out nicely.

"Think they'll call him in?" Matt was scowling as he reached for a cleaning cloth. Given the thick layer of dirt the crop sprayer had picked up it was a futile gesture, but it helped him relax.

"I hope not." Rose worried a fingernail. "Having two pilots really made a difference up here, and the emergency services are pretty happy with us so far." She waited a moment, shrugged and grabbed another cleaning cloth to help. They had been listening on the emergency channel during the last flight, and Matt was not the only one who needed a distraction. The situation with the fires had grown worse overnight, as new blazes were reported and others combined. Rob had not phoned since the day before, probably already airborne somewhere out in the thick of it, and the flying club were carefully avoiding the subject. No one wanted to upset Matt.

When Jim came out a few minutes later he was grinning.

"Well?" Rose demanded, scrubbing industriously at something that had once been a leaf.

"All done. They were calling the crews on standby and cancelling leave to assist with

149

the fire, but since I'm already working with the emergency services I've been told to carry on. Apparently I'm more use in the thick of it than lounging around in a uniform waiting for a signal."

"Probably got more than a few on base doing that already." Matt added sagely, and Jim chuckled in agreement.

"Won't that leave your crew short?" Rose asked.

"Nope, with all the fires they're just assembling crews from the people who can make it in. So how long until we can get the lovely Seaspray, who just saved me from hauling my arse into work, back into the air?" He was being deliberately enthusiastic, trying to conceal his nerves, but his exuberance failed to draw a reaction from Matt.

"Thirty minutes at least, probably an hour. Filling the water tank's slow going, no matter how quickly you manage to empty it." Rose's comment was irritated, and Jim cast around hastily for another topic. He seized on the first thing that came to mind.

"Matt, do you have a silhouette book?"

"In the hangar. Shelf by the door." The crop sprayer pilot's voice was muffled as he bent double to examine the aircraft's flaps.

"Thanks." Jim headed in, looking for the book, trying to resolve something that had been bothering him since the gorge. He was trained in silhouette recognition, and knew he should know this, although he tried to excuse himself on the grounds that the roaring fire below the aircraft had been extremely distracting. The shape of a white biplane, even coated in soot, should be a simple one to identify, and it was irritating him that he could not place it.

"Looking for anything in particular?" Matt asked. It was more interest than he had shown in most things since the incident of the day before and Jim did not want to discourage him.

"Bi-plane. A big white one with a stupidly low stall speed." He flicked through, looking increasingly frustrated.

"Terry Sacorski's Antonov?" Matt suggested, still looking over the crop sprayer. Jim flicked to the A's and quickly found what he was looking for.

"An AN-2?" he exclaimed, surprised.

"Yeah. Must have missed his party piece. Points it into a strong headwind and flies backwards." Matt's tone was completely matter-of-fact and Rose blinked, uncertain if he was joking. Jim did not respond, his head still buried in the book.

"Where's he flying from?" Matt asked.

"He said Lakeside," Jim replied, still reading, and Matt sucked his breath in.

"That's trouble then. He's only allowed to fly from his home field."

"Where's that? I haven't seen it flying around here." Jim looked up quickly.

"South east of Lydford." Matt stopped short, and then added "'Airfield on fire' is a good excuse, I guess." His voice was utterly flat, and Jim had the horrible feeling he had said something wrong. Rose obviously agreed as she coughed to draw his attention.

"Jim? Why don't you have a look in the hangar for a faster pump?"

"Err, yeah." Jim took the hint and headed in, putting the book back carefully on the shelf. He had a brief look through Matt's spares crates but all he managed to achieve was getting his hands dirty. As he well knew, if Matt had had a better pump it would already have been in use, and Jake's water tender would not be parked by the runway. It was no surprise to him when Rose slipped in a moment later and gestured she wanted a quiet word. Looking round, his eyes lit on the only private place in the hangar, and he pointed up the ladder and into the Shackleton. Staring at him in disbelief, Rose carefully climbed up and into the big aircraft. Once inside she looked round with some trepidation. Jim gestured her towards the back of the aircraft and quietly eased the door to the crew compartment closed behind them. Rose looked around doubtfully at the shabby leather and scrubbed metal that Matt was so carefully restoring, but seated herself on a box labelled 'Spares' and began.

"You're expecting too much from Matt. Stop trying to cheer him up and let him work through it."

"Look, it's just not right." Jim sat down heavily opposite her. "People die in this job. You can't let it get to you."

"It's not his job." Rose met his eyes squarely as he looked up in shock. "You're in the military, so you know you might have to kill or be killed. You've lost colleagues to accidents and Acts of God. Jake's a fire fighter. He's had to

153

deal with casualties and fatalities. He may not like it, but he's trained to deal with it. Matt's a pilot who took up crop dusting to fill his retirement. The very first time it came down to it, he couldn't save the people he was trying to. That's going to hit anyone hard." She had been ticking points off on her fingers as she spoke and Jim nodded, eyes wide in understanding. Crop spraying was one of the most dangerous forms of flying, but most deaths were the pilots, not people they were protecting on the ground.

"You know, dear? You are absolutely right."

"I usually am." She smiled briefly as he gave her a peck on the cheek.

"So what do I do about it? I want to help but –" He stared at the floor, swallowing hard. "I mean, what do you do in these situations?"

"Be your normal self. If Matt wants something, I'm sure he'll growl at you." Rose looked at him innocently and then her composure slipped and she began to chuckle. The pair of them began to laugh.

"Come on. We'd better head out, or Matt'll get suspicious." Jim stood. Inside the aircraft he knew, he felt strangely reassured. He looked the Shackleton over on the inside. Half finished, with parts of the structure exposed and the crew positions containing mostly taped-up or removed components, he could not see any rust. Matt really had done a spectacular job on her.

Rose paused, obviously about to say something and then changed her mind and started a different topic as she climbed down the ladder.

"Why are they calling the military in?" she asked, as he followed her out of the aircraft.

"Law and order. There's a lot of empty houses, and they've just had the first reports of looting."

"Oh for pity's sake." Her utterly disgusted tone echoed what Jim felt about the matter. People fleeing for their lives, leaving everything behind, and now they had to worry about opportunist thieves. His brother could go on for hours about fire crews having to risk themselves to rescue criminals from dangerous areas. Jim was more concerned about when the looters came armed, and if the Vale itself would be a target.

"Oy. You two!" Matt's sudden shout brought them out of the hangar. They were expecting a problem with the crop sprayer, but

155

instead he gestured to the road with distaste. A small car was making its way up to the airport, and Matt glowered as it turned up the trail towards the hangar. "See what they want."

The Stilsons lived on the southwest side of the Brooke's Vale where the hills rose slightly before turning into the steep rise and rocky outcroppings that formed the south border of the valley. They were a few of the people in the valley he did not get on with. When the Shackleton arrived, Julia Stilson had made several disparaging remarks about glorifying war, bombs, and implements of destruction. Matt had sent her running with pithy comments about people who did not know their aircraft, asked why she disapproved of search and rescue and pointed out that the only thing this particular aeroplane had ever dropped in its long service career was a lifeboat. Since this had all occurred in public, loudly, relationships with the Stilsons had been somewhat strained afterwards. Matt did not care. No one insulted his planes, and they were not customers anyway.

Unfortunately, after the events of the previous day, he was too drained to think about tormenting her as usual and settled for turning his back and walking into the hangar. Rose and Jim could deal with whatever the visitors wanted. If he had waited a moment longer he would have seen Jake parking his car behind them.

"Hi." Jim greeted them, looking round uncertainly.

"Don't see you up here often. What's up?" Rose added. The Stilsons looked at each other as Jake walked up to join them.

"We've found a problem in the valley." Mike Stilson began.

"A fire?" Jim reacted instantly, and his exclamation brought Matt back to the hangar door.

"No. Calm down." Jake's voice carried across as he covered the last stretch to the group. "But it's something we thought you might be able to help with. Did you know the landlines are out again?"

"We've been using mobile." Rose shrugged apologetically. "We hadn't noticed."

"At our end of the valley there's no mobile reception," Mike Stilson said. "Effectively we're cut off."

"Since you're working with the emergency services we wondered if there was

157

anything you could do. Rose, any engineering solutions?" Jake asked. Rose gave him a confused look.

"I'm not supposed to tamper with the phone network, and if the cable's out it won't work anyway. This has happened before and you weren't asking me to fix it, so what's different this time?" She drummed her fingers on the aircraft's wing, looking at them and waiting for an answer. Julia threw an uncertain look at Matt, who was waiting silently by the hangar, and then spoke.

"Look, the last we heard the fire front is closer to Brooke's Vale than it's ever been. The cable's out, either burned through or shut down. No phone, no web, no TV. The satellite signals aren't getting through the ash cloud, and interference is making the radio unusable. How do we know if an evacuation signal is sent?" Julia's question stopped them dead. Jake grimaced.

"We could evacuate everyone now, but that's just adding to the problem of displaced people," he began and Julia cut him off.

"And I'm not leaving my home unless we're ordered to." Her face was set, and her husband nodded his agreement. Jake shrugged, looking at the flying club.

"And that's the root of it. Matt? Anything here to help?"

"My scanner just receives. I use the aircraft radios for everything else."

"So we can get the signal in, but we'd need some kind of transmitter to distribute it to everyone else." Jim frowned thoughtfully.

"The transmitter would have to be inside the valley. The walls block most of the outside signals, and the ash is killing the rest," Julia said.

"Could we rig something up using an aerial?" Jake pondered slowly as he looked at his brother. "The church spire is high enough."

"Excuse me," Rose interrupted "but what we are looking for is a strong transmitter capable of sending a radio transmission on one frequency to the whole valley. Correct?"

"And strong enough to cut through the interference," Jim added.

"Ah." Rose nodded slowly. "What about the maritime patrol radio set you've got sitting inside that Shackleton in the hangar?" There was a slight pause as everyone looked at Matt expectantly. He shuffled.

"Does it work?" Jim pressed.

"It works fine." Matt looked at his feet. "I've been listening to the local traffic on it while I patch her up. Just forgot it sent as well." At Matt's embarrassed admission, there was a relieved chuckle from Jake.

"OK then, we have a transmitter. What about a frequency?"

"Pick anything commercial and not FM. We can't get them here at the moment anyway," Jim suggested.

"Fine. How about this?" Julia fished a card from her pocket. "My son's favourite. I can't stand it."

"No problem." Jake looked at the card and began to laugh out loud, getting some very odd looks. "Come on, we're drowning out a classic metal station with an Avro Shackleton."

"Right, so how do we do this?" Jim tried to get the conversation back on track, aware that he had missions to fly later.

"Well," Rose gestured to the map. "According to the contour lines, the airfield's as good a place for a radio as any."

"Planned it that way," Matt interrupted, stabbing a finger at a spot by the runway. "If we can put her here it'll help. Otherwise the hangar will block half of it."

"So we'll hook the SUV up and tow her out." Mike Stilson suggested and Matt stared at him. Both the twins sniggered.

"Empty, that plane weighs at least twenty tons. I think your SUV might have problems," Jim replied, less than diplomatically.

"We can just fire up a couple of the engines and roll her out under her own steam," Matt pronounced with careful civility, trying to keep them on track without provoking an argument with Julia.

"Tell you what," Jake cut in, before the discussion could go any further. "Julia, Mike, could you go home, tune into the radio and wait? Once we've got it up and running we'll give you a signal to send us, since we can see your house from here. Then once it's working, can you go round and start telling everyone else?"

"We'll stop in on the Taverners on the way and warn them about the engine noise," Julia added, and the Stilsons turned to walk down to their car, grateful for something to do. As they left, Matt looked at the others. Having a task to complete seemed to be bringing him out of his depression, or at least distracting him.

"Well, we're going to need the very long fuel hose. Might do it on two engines, might get her out on one. Why are you standing around? Get cracking!"

"Wait a minute!" Jim protested. "At least let me get on my way before you start moving that monster around!"

"Fine. Then we get everything set up ready for after you've gallivanted off in my plane."

"Aren't you going to need a few people to help with starting her?" It was as close as Jim could venture to mentioning that the aircraft usually needed a team of at least five without betraying his familiarity with the plane.

"Where am I going to get 'em? I'll make do with Rose and Jake with fire extinguishers, just in case."

Leaving Jim and Rose to manage the crop sprayer, Matt headed towards the hangar. Rubbing his hands together, he wrapped the hangar door handle in a cloth and got a grip with both fists. With a solid heave, dirt grinding beneath it as the door moved in its channel, the sliding door opened back, continued passed the normal opening until fully half the hangar front was exposed. Jake got a grip on the other side and with some difficulty pulled the second door fully back, dropping the deadbolt into its hole in the ground to secure it. He stepped back into the hangar, looking at the shape the sunlight was just reaching at the back.

"Wow. It's the giant mutant brother of a Lancaster." Jake looked at Matt for a reaction, but did not expect the one he got. Matt looked over his prized aircraft, raised an eyebrow and nodded before he walked towards the ladder leading up inside. Jake took a step back, leaving Matt to deal with his plane, and turned to Rose and Jim. He tapped on Rose's shoulder to get her attention without shouting something Matt could hear.

"Matt's definitely not himself. I insulted the Shack, and he just nodded at me."

"What did you say?" Rose asked, exasperated. He told her, and the expression on her face dissolved into that of someone trying not to laugh. Across the crop duster wing, Jim nodded and looked at him sagely.

"You're quite right."

"What?" Jake paused thrown and Jim looked at him.

"Same company, designer, factories, manufacturer. Giant mutant stepdaughter might be closer, but you're on the right lines. Remember, planes are always girls." The pilot lectured his brother, in the tone of someone talking to a particularly dim child.

"And pilots are always nuts." Jake shook his head at the pair of them and decided to chalk it up to experience.

A faint shout drew their attention. Jill was waving from the house door, clutching a folded map. Rose looked at the pair and then sighed and wandered down to see what she wanted. As the two women vanished inside, Jake looked at Jim with a raised eyebrow.

"Aircraft are always girls?" He queried, sensing an unsaid caveat.

"Except when they're bitches." Jim threw a sour glance at the Dromader, and then chuckled slightly. "That's unfair of me. It's actually handled really well under awful flying conditions." Out of the corner of Jim's eye he caught sight of Matt standing just inside the hangar watching them, and thanked all the deities he knew of that he had added the disclaimer.

"So, is Matt going to turn you into a crop sprayer pilot then?" Jake teased, and Jim shook his head vigorously.

"Nope. I like planes with redundant engines. They're my type of girl."

"Does Rose know she's got competition?" Jake said slyly, nodding as Rose stepped out of the front door and began to walk across. His brother glared at him, but wisely did not respond.

"Jim, your next run. I don't think this is something you've done before." Rose was carrying a large map book, folded round a sheet of notes, and Jim's heart sunk.

"Go on."

"Can you spray down this area?" She opened the book. The first thing that struck him were the contour lines, which looked as though someone had dragged a comb around on the page. The next was the large industrial area right by the field. He swallowed.

"What exactly do they want me to do?"

"Well, the field has irrigation channels, due to the steepness. To avoid wasting water you will need to follow the channels exactly, to ensure the water does not run down the hill to the electricity station at the bottom." Jim blinked. "Of course, because of the electricity station there are a number of low wires in the area, but you can't risk knocking them down, so you'll need to fly underneath them. And then there's the railway bridge…"

"You're kidding."

"Yeah I am actually. They want you to do that field by the Lowry Road they assigned you this morning, before they sent you to the canyon. Just dump the water parallel to the roadside and as close as you can get it." She smiled at him innocently and Jim gave her a cold look, before it was replaced with a calculating glare and a glance from side to side that settled on the hosepipe by the hangar. She saw the look and stepped back holding the map book up in mock defence. "Don't you dare! You have a mission to complete."

"Fine, but when I get back, you owe me for that," Jim threatened.

"I'll hold you to that." She grinned. "Take care up there, OK?"

"Yeah."

"Jim, a tip for you." Matt walked across and pulled himself up onto the wing, leaning into the cockpit. He pointed to the little control. "Remember your trim adjust. She's a completely manual system, so you'll have to tweak her more than you're used to, but without managing the trim she's a nightmare to control."

Jim's eyes widened as he realised his mistake. The trim tabs, small flaps along the edges of the aircraft's control surfaces, were designed to take some of the load off the pilot. On a short flight with no real complications, like his initial trips round the valley, the trim had only needed occasional adjustments. With the more complex flying he was doing now the aircraft would need regular adjustments as her handling changed with speed, conditions and the varying weight in the tank.

"Thanks Matt."

"Don't thank me. I want my plane back in one piece!" The characteristic snarl showed that Matt was at least partly back to his old self, and brought grins from his audience. Distinctly unimpressed by their reaction, Matt jumped down from the wing and gestured Jim imperiously into the cockpit. "Now, get out there and don't disgrace me!"

Rose watched the crop sprayer take off and smiled slightly. Jill had been looking after Matt all morning. It had been Rose, not Jill, manning the radio and Rose who had heard, heart in mouth, the transmissions between the aircraft over the canyon. Before Jim returned she had had just enough time to ask Matt what an air pocket was.

"Dead air," he had answered, distracted. "Somewhere an aircraft just won't fly. Hit one, and you might drop a hundred feet or a couple of thousand before you get lift back. Hellova shock when it happens."

She had gone into the hangar and composed herself, knowing that until this was over the last thing she could do was tell Jim. The extra stress was a distraction he did not need while he was flying in these conditions. It was hard, knowing that he was risking his life while there was nothing she could do. She reflected to herself that if she married him, this was what it would mean to be a military wife and wondered if she would be up to it. For now however, she had a Shackleton to move and a radio station to set up.

In the cockpit Jim watched the entrance to Brooke's Vale pass underneath him. The crop sprayer was handling perfectly, light on the controls and behaving predictably, as she usually did in straight level flight and good conditions. Remembering Matt's advice he checked the trim, loosening his grip on the stick to see if it pulled. Nothing unusual, but then she only seemed to play up at low levels or turbulence. It had to be something he was doing wrong, which meant Matt was probably right about the trim.

A quick look at the GPS revealed a series of fields between him and his target location. He thought for a moment and then shrugged to himself. As long as he avoided power lines he should be fine to test a few things out. A few simulated runs might reveal what the issue was, and get some practice for the live run so he did not embarrass himself too badly. With that cheerful thought, fingers on the trim control, he put the crop sprayer into a dive.

Inside the hangar, the Shackleton had been half hidden by the shadows and the dim light. Now, as it turned slowly on the grass beside the runway in the full glare of the summer sun, Rose gained a new appreciation of the size of Matt's pet project. Her ears rang from the growl of the engines, as the monstrous aircraft rolled out of the hangar and onto the tarmac. With skilled precision, Matt taxied it off the strip and positioned it carefully by the runway. Now she and the others watched, safely out of the way on the far side of the airfield, as the propellers spun to a stop. They had only run two of the engines, but that was quite loud enough.

"Weird looking isn't it?" Jake commented.

"Four engines, eight propellers." She shook her head. "It's one thing Matt saying they turn in opposite directions, it's quite another to see it. Like that, on one shaft – the gearing must be amazing."

"Yeah, and to hear Matt tell it, really temperamental." He was talking to the back of her head as she walked across. Matt had opened the fuselage door and climbed out on the ladder.

"Chocks!" he bellowed, looking round. Jake and Rose grabbed the large metal wedges from the hangar and shoved them into place against the wheels. They struggled with the weight but Matt did not help, standing back with folded arms and surveying his pride and joy.

"Wow. Our own radio station." Jake gasped, out of breath. "Anyone want to tell Jill what all the noise was?"

"Yes, please do." Jill was standing outside the house, arms folded. "Matt are you planning something stupid? You're not that desperate to fly, are you?"

"No. Just setting up a radio in case we need to send out an emergency signal. Do you want to make the first transmission from Radio Shackleton?" Matt asked, politely gesturing to the ladder. Jill looked at it, and then down at her skirt.

"Matt, why don't you do the honours? I need to change."

"I'll look after the scanner for you," Rose offered, walking down to the house. Jill nodded gratefully and turned to cut through the woodland path that led back to her place.

"Nope. Rose get in here. Jake, you're on radio." Matt's comment stopped Rose dead.

"Why?" Jake asked, mock-warily. "Planning bad things with my brother's soon-to-be-fiancée?"

"She's got a better voice than you or me." Matt was still glaring from the top of the ladder, and Rose looked helplessly at Jake.

"Go on. I'll man the radio and listen in." Jake walked towards the house shaking his head, as Rose shrugged and climbed up.

"Why are you shouting?" she asked, and Matt glowered.

"Forgot my ear protection. I'm a little deaf. Turn right. It's down the front." Carefully she did so and stopped, looking into the crew compartment. The crew seats were placed facing across the fuselage, consoles mounted on the wall, and a narrow space behind them left to walk down. Two raised sections ran across the middle, separating two of the seats.

"Wing spars," Matt said laconically, as Rose looked at them.

"You want Jill to climb over those? She's going to love this," Rose commented, and walked in before he could respond. She scrambled carefully over the first raised section, then gave up, sat on the next one, pulled her feet up, pivoted round on her rear and stood up. "So where do I sit and what do I do?"

With a few adjustments, and Matt's reserve batteries hooked up for power, the radio was ready to go. After some heated debate it had been decided to stick with a short broadcast every hour on the hour with the fire's location, the crop sprayer's latest mission and the valley status. Any evacuation order would be broadcast the moment it was received, and repeated frequently. Within the valley the Shackleton's powerful radio should cut through the interference like a knife. The only faint concern was how far outside the valley it could be received, but since there was no other way to ensure that word got out if an evacuation was ordered in the valley, that issue was shelved.

"This is Radio Shackleton broadcasting to Brooke's Vale. Since we've lost main radio we will be broadcasting any emergency signals on this channel. Test signal to the Stilsons, Matt's watching with binoculars. Can you open and close your attic window three times?" Rose's transmission went out, and she turned the radio off, removing the heavy headset Matt had supplied. Since getting in and out was so awkward she was not leaving until he told her it was successful.

Standing by the hangar, looking out over the valley, Matt didn't need the binoculars. A moment after the transmission the light flashed off the Stilsons' attic window, as the frame moved and it reflected the sunlight towards them. He continued to watch as it flashed again, lowering. From the other side of the valley another glint caught his eye and he raised his binoculars curiously. The Taverners had opened their own roof window and were looking across at the Stilsons' house. Absentmindedly he noted a third flash of light as the Stilsons lowered their window for the second time, but now he was looking round the valley with his binoculars. It took him a moment to spot Roger Barnehurst, standing at his landing window also clutching a pair of binoculars and looking at the Stilsons. The Hughes family were standing on their front lawn looking up at the house. Further across the valley, Claude Sampson was standing on his balcony, drink in hand, and watching the proceedings with a smile before he raised his glass towards the airfield. Matt shook his head in amazement. It seemed the Stilsons really had got the word out.

Jake stuck his head out of the door of the house and gave a thumbs up before he ventured out.

"All OK, so whoever wants to take over here, please do. I've got my own job to do."

"Thanks." Matt rapped on the underside of the fuselage. "Oy! All OK."

Inside the Shackleton Rose paused a moment and had a sudden thought. She put the headset back on and then thumbed the transmit for one extra message.

"This is Radio Shackleton. Test successful. Updates will be every hour on the hour from now on. Out." Grinning to herself she put the headset on the seat and went down to join the others. Radio Shackleton was live.

Jim whistled to himself as he flew back towards Brooke's Vale. The drop had gone well, even if he said so himself. A few low passes over abandoned fields on the way had helped. He had used the opportunity to practice manipulating the trim; adjusting the settings until he found one he could live with for the low level sweeps. Then he had climbed back to cruising height, raised his airspeed, and promptly had to adjust it again. At least he felt more confident with the adjustments going into the run. Matt would probably critique him for playing with the trim, but he was still getting used to how frequently to adjust it. On the other hand, if he had to choose between Matt's moaning and his own sore legs, arms and back, his ears could take the strain. After all, the results of the flight had been a successful firebreak, and that was all that mattered.

Turning towards the target, lining up parallel to the road, he had given himself a long run up to adjust speed and approach. To his great satisfaction when he hit the dump the water had neatly covered the edge of the field, part of the road and the ditch that ran between them. With the runoff from the tarmac the ditch should be nicely filled, its ends blocked to make a temporary stream. The gully, the canyon, and now the road. Jim grinned to himself. He was getting good at making firebreaks, as long as he had a large enough target.

The Vale was less than three minutes away when his phone vibrated. Checking for other aircraft he saw none, and risked a quick looked down. Two words were displayed from Rose: "Call me" and the Brooke's Vale regional frequency. Puzzled and worried he changed the frequency and transmitted.

"C-SPRY 10 to Brooke's Vale. Are you receiving?" He listened anxiously and the response came almost immediately.

"Brooke's Vale to C-SPRY 10. Emergency Diversion Request. It's the Rookery

Lodge. There are people trapped there. Six evacuees."

"C-SPRY 10 to Brooke's Vale. I can't take them. This is a two seater." Jim signalled back, privately wondering if Rose had lost her mind, and more to the point how she was managing to transmit. The valley did not have a radio with this range on it. Then he chuckled to himself. It looked like the Shack was up and running.

"Brooke's Vale to C-SPRY 10. There's another aircraft on the way. The rear lawns are long enough for you take take-off and land if your tank's empty. Watch for the slope. Ask the Emergency guys. Out." Jim flicked back to the emergency channel, wondering what on earth was going on.

"C-SPRY 10 to Base," he signalled. "Querying request to pick up from Rookery Lodge?"

"Base to C-SPRY 10. Confirmed. E-VAC 24 is already on site. Co-ordinate with him." Jim acknowledged, changing his route rather than heading home.

The Rookery was not hard to reach from here, but his heart sank at the smoke rising ahead of him. One of the smaller fires was closing on the Lodge, but from what Matt had said it would only take one spark for the place to go up. He could see no sign of the area Matt had sprayed yesterday, and shook his head at how quickly it had dried out. The wide lawns he had been directed to land on looked like straw, and he silently gave thanks for the well and stream that fed Brooke's Vale. Low though they were, they had kept the valley green, perhaps even damp enough to stop the fire getting a foothold if it reached them.

He did one quick pass to gauge his landing space, and spotted a small aircraft with a group of people standing by it. Their conversation had stopped, and they were all looking up. He shook his head again in disbelief. There were more than six there, and he could only take one. The air in front of him was rippling, and he knew that he could see the heat haze from the fire. It decided him.

Swiftly he swung around for another pass, and came in to land. He was leaving enough room to taxi towards the other aircraft, but had a nervous eye on the group by it. Panicking people did stupid things, and if one of them ran into the path of the crop sprayer they could do enough damage to ground it, killing themselves in the process.

As the wheels touched and bumped, he turned the aircraft to taxi, noting with relief that they had stayed where they were. He brought the aircraft to a halt, leaving himself plenty of room from the other plane. Even as Jim opened the door, another man was running across, leading a woman who was holding a toddler. He gave the propeller a wide berth and leaned into the cockpit. Jim braced himself to say he could only take one passenger, expecting an argument, and then looked across.

"Rob!" His face fell. "We can't secure the baby. It's not safe if we crash."

"She's not safe here either." The mother's response was surprisingly calm. "I'll hold her."

"Ok. Climb in, but keep off the control surfaces on the wing. Seat's rear-facing. Put the headset on." Jim gave in quickly, remembering the heat haze over the rise. "Rob the fire's just over the hill. Turn away on take off and watch for the thermals."

"Gotcha." The other pilot shut the cockpit, and dashed back to his own aircraft. Quickly he began marshalling the remaining passengers into the Robin. Behind Jim, the woman was seated, securing the belt firmly around herself and holding the toddler on her lap sideways, arms and legs tucked in tightly. Mercifully the child was not crying, looking around with wide terrified eyes, afraid because her mother was.

"Ready and belted. I've got a good grip on her," the woman said, quietly. The headset was obviously already on, settled with professional speed.

"Hold her tight," Jim growled. This did not sit well with him, but he saw no other choice. He increased throttle and turned the aircraft, giving himself as much space as possible to take off. The crop sprayer's limitations were cabin space rather than weight, but with an unrestrained passenger he wanted a smooth take off and as much space for error as possible. He was breaking every safety rule in the book but he could not, in conscience, leave people to burn.

Behind him the passengers were silent, and he pressed the throttle, crushing the country club's dry lawns beneath the wheels as the aircraft accelerated. Pushing forward on the stick he lowered the nose, putting the crop sprayer into the right angle for take off. He focused on what he could feel through the seat, peering at the ground ahead for any bumps or ridges that could launch the crop sprayer prematurely into the air in a high painful bounce. Staring at the approaching edge of the field as the aircraft's speed continued to increase, Jim lowered the nose further wondering if he was raising the tail too far, and then the crop sprayer was lifting away smoothly. His slight sigh was echoed, but he ignored it, banking as sharply as he dared to turn away from the fire and clear the airspace for the other aircraft.

On the Rookery lawn, the Robin was beginning its own run. The little aircraft had its third wheel under the nose, not the tail, and that brought its own problems on the rough ground. Weighed down as it was, Rob would have to get as much speed as he could on the ground then rotate, allowing the aircraft to climb away. If he got it wrong the Robin would fail to climb, falling back to the ground in a bounce that would cost them valuable runway – and could damage the aircraft badly.

The Robin rolled forward and round in a loop that brought it close to the edge of the field, aiming to get the longest run possible. It was already accelerating as Rob entered the straight run to take off, angled towards the field's far corner to gain as much space as he could. Obviously overloaded, the small aircraft initially seemed to flounder across the grass, but as it gained speed, control and grace came with it. Still accelerating, it was now most of the way across the lawns and still had not lifted. Jim was not sure if it could not, or if Rob was holding off to get some extra speed, and then finally the Robin lifted into a shallow climb. Reluctant as he was to distract the other pilot, Jim could see more from his higher altitude and thumbed the radio on the community channel.

"Rob, turn left forty degrees. Fire's closing from the East." There was no acknowledgement, but the other aircraft obviously heard as the pilot banked left shallowly, turning away from the flames.

"Go to the emergency channel." The terse message came back and Jim complied.

"...clear. Low on fuel, can't make set down. Need alternative." As he heard Rob's message, Jim paused then hit his own transmission, feeling oddly self-conscious on the official channel.

"C-SPRY 10 to E-VAC 24. Suggest you head for Brooke's Vale." He was already turning as he transmitted, suddenly aware that the fire behind them was still a threat. Sweeping in, driven by the wind, the smoke and ash clouds before it were dangerous to aircraft. Large fire fighting aircraft were buffeted and blown; the two small aircraft up here would be tossed like toys and overloaded as it was the Robin would not be able to handle it.

"E-VAC 24 and C-SPRY 10 on course to Brooke's Vale." The relieved voice on the radio told him that Rob had the same idea: to move as far from the fire as quickly as possible. Both aircraft broke for their home airfield, aware that behind them the fire was gathering pace as the wind drove it after them.

It was a horrible thought, but Jim knew the crop sprayer's top speed was only about one hundred and forty miles per hour. The Robin, particularly overladen as it was, was not much faster. He could not remember how fast a forest fire could move, just that it was faster than cars and running men. He knew he could lift away and still stand a chance, but the little wooden aircraft in the air next to him was vulnerable to red ash and heat. If either of them were forced down he would not give much for their chances.

"F-101 to E-VAC 24. Are you clear?" The new voice addressing them was a surprise. Jim did not know what they were asking, but the answer came back from Rob.

"E-VAC 24 to F-101. E-VAC and C-SPRY 10 are clear."

"F-101 to E-VAC 24, we have visual on you. Keep going."

A shadow fell across the cockpit of the crop sprayer, and as Jim looked round, a second later it moved across the Robin and onwards. Whatever had cast it was behind them, and large.

Carefully, keeping an eye on the Robin, Jim turned course slightly to give him a view, cursing the lack of mirrors in Matt's crop sprayer. Behind him the red shape of a Canadair water bomber lifted one wingtip in a turn to line it up for a second run. As it began the run down the line of the fire, where the forest met the Rookery lawns it dropped its cargo in a single spray that saturated the land. The Canadair was being tossed and buffeted, but the pilot held it steady, turned and completed a third pass. Made tiny by the distance, its tanks emptied, the large aircraft lifted away. Climbing, it turned to travel round to base to reload. Its parting transmission did not inspire confidence.

"F-101 to base. Firebreak unsuccessful." Jim blinked a moment. If a fire-fighting aircraft like the Canadair could not turn back the fire front, Matt and the crop sprayer had stood no chance at Pine Lees.

"Why couldn't they have picked us up?" The quiet voice from behind him reminded him that he had passengers.

"Not enough space to take off and land," he said bluntly.

"Oh." She nodded to herself, apparently forgetting that he could not see her.

"You seem to be taking this very calmly." Jim regretted his comment at once. If the passenger was going to crack or act up, and the forest fire had easily provided enough stress for that, a question like that could trigger it. He would much prefer breakdowns occurred on the ground, whether it were planes or people.

"We were going to draw straws." From the tone he could tell she had smiled slightly, faintly as she answered. Jim's mouth went dry. There really was not much to say to that. Instead he thumbed the radio as the rise at the start of the valley came into view.

"C-SPRY 10 to E-VAC 24, how are you for fuel?"

"E-VAC 24 to C-SPRY 10. Running low. Mind if I land first?"

"C-SPRY 10 to E-VAC 24. Go ahead."

Beside them the little Robin dropped into an approach run. Rob was giving himself plenty of space to pull up and go round if anything went wrong, keeping the approach shallow. With more passengers than seatbelts, a rough approach could turn an unrestrained passenger into a missile in the cabin.

The Robin touched down lightly almost at the start of the runway, and Rob gave it a long run to slow down, reducing speed smoothly along the tarmac. With an ease that told of the pilot's familiarity with his aircraft, and this airstrip, there were no bounces, just the single touch and a smooth run off. Jim shot a quick look round, worried about the toddler, and realised he would have to do the same for his own landing. He could not see the child, but suspected she was beginning to fidget on her mother's lap.

"E-VAC 24 to C-SPRY 10. Brooke's Vale Runway is clear." Rob's signal let Jim know it was his turn. He swallowed, slightly nervous. Completely unintentionally, Rob had given him a hard act to follow.

"Make sure you have a very good hold on her," Jim advised his passenger, and then lined up for his own run.

"C-SPRY 10 beginning approach run at Brooke's Vale," he reported, and then as gently as he could he brought the plane in. Consciously he followed Rob's method with a shallow approach to the runway, but even so it was not as smooth. The aircraft bounced twice and then he felt the rumble through the wheels that told him she was down. He pulled her in well clear of the Robin and stopped the engine.

In the plane beside them the Robin's passengers were beginning to climb out. Rob was directing them carefully over the wing and down the to ground, and Jim remembered his own passenger as he heard her begin to undo the straps.

"If you want me to –" he began, and then stopped. She was already turning round to get out. He climbed out and offered a hand down, which she accepted gratefully, and then she was walking towards the little Robin, toddler in hand. Beyond them, he could see one of the men by the Robin turn, and say something, before he smiled and scooped up the little toddler. An undemonstrative couple perhaps, but the father was holding the child as if he thought she would vanish. Beyond them Jim could see the Robin. Three people were already out, and as a fourth passenger stepped out, and another head popped up in the back seat Jim had to laugh. The whole thing reminded him of nothing so much as one of the old clowns in a car routine.

He climbed out himself, aware that Rose had connected the water hose, and was working on the fuel. Jill was nowhere to be seen, probably fixing food and showers for their evacuees, if she was not ferrying the doctor up to see them.

It appeared six passengers was Rob's limit in the four-seater. As the last one climbed out the young pilot secured the cabin and then jumped down himself, walking across to Jim.

"Hey, Rob in the Robin!" Jim's greeting was an old joke and brought a grin from the other pilot.

"Sorry about the rush. I didn't know who C-SPRY 10 was until you'd landed. Hey, Uncle Matt." He waved at Matt, who had emerged from the hangar, wiping grease off his hands. The older pilot looked over the evacuees and for a moment his face went blank. Then he composed himself and the moment passed.

"Let's see to the guests first shall we? Youth of today, no manners." He snorted as he strolled across. "Welcome to the hangar at Brooke's Vale. If you want to come indoors we've got some food, showers and a place to rest while we get the planes refuelled. And who is this pretty young lady?" He herded them off towards the mobile home that functioned as an office and extra space at the hangar. Rob watched bemused.

"What's wrong with Uncle Matt?"

"Had a family killed in front of him yesterday. He won't talk about it." Jim's voice was utterly flat, but Rob's silent nod told him he understood. He could not help but wonder if the other pilot had similar experiences to relate from the evacuations. Awkwardly Jim cast around for another subject, but Rob cut him off.

"What is that doing out?" Rob was staring at the side of the runway and the huge grey shape of the Shackleton. Jim blinked and then started to laugh as Rose smirked and gestured with a flourish.

189

"Let me present Radio Shackleton, broadcasting to Brooke's Vale. We're doing hourly bulletins and updates where we can." Rose grinned at Rob's obvious confusion.

"But why? How?"

"We lost most phone and communications. Radio and TV are out. Mobiles aren't working. Julia pointed out that half the valley would never hear an evacuation order, and we've all got friends to worry about."

"Makes sense." Rob admitted slowly, and then stopped. "Has anyone told Jill how the radio works?"

"Matt's given her pre-sets." Rose sniggered slightly, and Jim joined in, adding his own opinion.

"Believe me Rob, her face was a picture when Matt sat her in front of the system and told her that was the new radio."

"I can believe it." Rob looked completely stunned and Jim took pity on him, turning the conversation back to something easier to manage.

"So you're E-VAC 24 eh? I guess I know who to listen out for."

"Yeah. We're not doing anything exciting, just evacuation runs. It's pretty much the farmsteads with fields. It lets the emergency crews use the helicopters and big evac aircraft where they're really needed." Rob was rambling a bit, and as Jim watched he realised the young pilot's eyes were slightly unfocused.

"Rob, you're exhausted."

"I'll be fine, it's just – " He swayed, the adrenaline leaving his system after the close call at the Rookery. Jim caught his arm.

"Yeah right. It'll take time to refuel the planes. Why don't you get some sleep, we can talk later." Rob tried to protest but Jim cut him off. "Look, I'll wake you when it's fuelled."

The last statement was a complete lie. Although there were several more hours flying time available that day, Jim had no intention of letting Rob fly in his current condition. However, as far as Jim was concerned, Rob did not need to know that. As Rose set the Robin up to refuel, Jim guided Rob into the office where a small couch had been set up as a bed. Rob collapsed onto it gratefully, and then his eyes opened again.

"Don't you need sleep?"

"I used to fly long duration missions," Jim said with a faint grin, and then realised his mistake. "And Matt and I are swapping pilot duties."

Rob's eyes had already closed as he finished, and Jim slipped out closing the door quietly behind him.

He stretched carefully, trying to ease cramped muscles. While Jim had spent longer in the cockpits of other aircraft, the crop sprayer really was not built with the pilot's comfort in mind. He wondered idly if this was why Matt had agreed so readily when he first suggested swapping flying duties. Rob had definitely had the right idea taking the Robin before he could end up on crop sprayer duty.

Rose waved laconically to him from the side of the Robin, watching the fuel pump with a bored expression, and he went over to join her. He had always liked the Robin, with its upturned wings and almost 360-degree field of view. The fact it was an easy plane to fly helped as well. Now the brown and white livery was in a state, ash marks and soot streaked across it. The underside was caked with mud and straw from the repeated grass landings, and the chocolate brown strip along her side was hardly visible under the crusting of yellow-grey dust.

Grabbing one of Matt's ever-present cleaning rags, he set to work on the worst of the dirt.

He had not got very far before Jill walked across to the planes, carrying a tray of sandwiches.

"No good you fainting while you work," she said, with a raised eyebrow, and Jim chuckled as he tucked in.

"You're a lifesaver. So what's the next mission?"

"Nothing on Seaspray yet, but we've had an update from the services about the Robin. They'd like the guys you just brought in flown down to Lakeside as soon as possible."

"Why?" Jim looked a little confused. "They're safe here. Wouldn't it make more sense to keep evacuating others?"

"Not quite. He's in air traffic control, she's a doctor – a burns specialist apparently. Not all the kids are theirs, and the other parents are at Lakeside so they want them reunited. It makes the paperwork easier."

"I suppose that makes sense. We're not going anywhere until the planes are refuelled, anyway. How's Matt?" Jim's concern was obvious. Jill looked at him for a moment, and then shook her head.

193

"Putting a brave face on it. He can move his hand a bit, so the glove's doing some good. At the moment he's hovering around the radio scanner."

"Why are you two still down at the house?" Jim asked, puzzled. "The Shackleton has a working radio."

"It also has an uncomfortable seat, no coffee facilities and dreadful mobile reception," Jill replied lifting an eyebrow. "I'm quite comfortable only using it to broadcast. Besides, that thing's been sitting in the sun for hours. Do you have any idea how hot it is?"

"Believe me, I can guess." Jim chuckled quietly. He could remember days when the aircraft had been too hot to touch and when climbing in and out of crew positions had been a matter of carefully not touching vulnerable flesh to scorching metal. "I notice you've ditched the skirt."

"Yes well, getting to the radio operator's seat in that cabin in a skirt is tricky. With all the work on refuelling and crawling around inside that greasy old plane, I thought I'd do better in my old gardening clothes. For a big plane, there's not a lot of space in there."

"How's Rose getting on with it then?" Jim took a quick guess, knowing his fiancée's obsession with all things mechanical, and was rewarded as Jill laughed. From the other side of the Robin an answering snigger told him that he had guessed correctly.

"Well, you were chatting to her earlier without any problems," Jill said, with a grin at Rose. Jim smiled broadly, his guess about how they had contacted him confirmed.

"I'd have called your mobile, but I didn't want to distract you," Rose admitted, from where she was keeping an eye on the Robin's refuelling and then scowled at the fuel pump. "Fuelling one plane at a time, doing both is going to take a while."

"Matt has got the fittings for a second fuel hose in the hangar somewhere," Jill said. "He usually only flies one aircraft, so he never set it up."

"Not worth starting it now," Rose decided. "This one'll be fuelled pretty quickly. Only another fifteen minutes or so."

"It'll take longer than that for Rob to be ready to fly." Jim coughed slightly as two concerned faces turned to him. "He's exhausted. I'd say medically unfit to fly."

"Then we'll have to delay flying them back." Jill looked disappointed. "Jim, would you be able to fly them?"

"Not without a break first." He shook his head, rolling a shoulder back to ease the nagging ache. "And even then I'm not sure. I don't know that plane well. She's an easy bird to fly, but I've never soloed her."

"Jill, could you fly it?" Rose asked, and the office manager grimaced.

"No. No instrument rating. If I get caught in a smoke cloud I'm in trouble. Besides apparently it's bedlam down at Lakeside. That kind of flying's beyond me."

"Then we'll have to wait for Rob," Jim said flatly. "And I'm not waking him."

"I'll tell Matt." Jill nodded in understanding, heading back to the house. "He can tell the Emergency Services. If it'll get him to stop stuffing sweets into that poor kid for five minutes, the delay will be worth it."

A few minutes passed and then Matt himself walked up. He peered carefully through the door of the office and nodded unsurprised, before he continued towards the planes. Stopping a way off, he looked the Robin over disapprovingly. Always fastidious about his aircraft, his opinion of the Robin's current condition was clear on his face.

"Matt?" Jim asked, and was dismissed with an irritated handwave.

"Just want to make sure she's in one piece." As the pump clicked dry, Rose jumped and went to disconnect it, finding herself observed very closely as she did so. Carefully she wiped the fuel rim and then replaced the cap, looking at Matt for approval.

"That OK?"

"Get on with the crop sprayer." The terse order brought a raised eyebrow from Rose, but she and Jim did as they were told. Meanwhile, Matt appeared to be going over the Robin with a fine tooth comb. Wings, rudder, flaps, propeller… Eventually he finished and stood clear, flexing his gloved hand thoughtfully. He looked at Jim, and then at the office where Rob was still out cold.

"I'll be flying the next runs," he commented flatly, and Jim didn't argue. In Rob's exhausted state it was obvious to both of them he should not be flying.

"Fine with me. Just remember you're E-VAC 24, and when you get back here watch for me. We don't want a collision."

"Agreed." If Matt was surprised at the lack of argument, he did not show it. There was a discreet cough from behind them, and both pilots turned. Jake was standing by the hangar door, holding a kit bag.

"Any room on one of those flights for me? They've called in the reserves so I volunteered."

"We're heading for Lakeside airport," Matt told him.

"That's where I need to go." Jake's expression was icily calm, and it was obvious he was not going to change his mind.

"It would be two trips anyway," Matt commented, rather than waste time talking him out of it. "You, her, the toddler and two kids. The rest in the second run. Rose, can you get them?" Rose nodded and headed towards the evacuees, throwing a quick worried look at Jake.

"Why so sombre? I thought you were a dangerous feminist who doesn't take orders!" Jake shot after her, trying to cheer her up. Unfortunately she was still close enough to reply. Rose stopped dead, walked back, and prodded him in the chest.

"No. It means I take orders from the person who is best for the job. I just expect the same courtesy back, when that's me. Despite what Roger thinks we're not all raving loonies, you know." Point made, she turned on her heel and walked off. Then she paused and looked back, concern plain on her face. "Take care of yourself out there OK? And that is an order."

Jake chuckled and nodded. Satisfied, she strode off to round up the evacuees.

"How's things with Rose?" Jake looked at Jim expectantly. His brother recognised the question as the last moments of human contact sought by those going into danger, just before they focused on the job. He had seen it in his own crew too often to snap at Jake for asking.

"Fine. We're just taking it slow." An arm looped out, wrapping firmly around his neck and pulling him close.

"A bit of brotherly advice. She's far too good for you, so if I were you, I'd propose before she comes to her senses. Because if you don't I'm going to go down on one knee, propose and tell her I'm you." Jake's statement was said quite calmly, and Jim shoved him off looking horrified.

"You wouldn't." He relaxed slightly. "Besides, she can tell us apart."

"Only if she wants to, little brother. Oh isn't that a nice sight?" Jake's grin was wide, more when he pointed to the object of their conversation walking back across the tarmac carrying the toddler and leading another child by the hand. The other passengers for this run were following.

"Take the hint OK? See you around." Jake ruffled his brother's hair, avoided the quick swipe Jim took as revenge and climbed into the Robin, getting himself settled and the bag stowed. With a poorly concealed smirk, Matt got the rest of his passengers loaded and comfortable.

Jim stood clear while the Robin took off. A hand slipped into his and he looked round, then hugged Rose gratefully as they watched the Robin lift away. As it levelled out and receded, Rose gave him a peck on the cheek, and then turned to the crop duster. He tried not to think that this could be the last time he saw his brother alive, and to convince himself that Jake would be all right. After all, the man had spent ten years on the front line of the fire service before he moved into the fire marshall's role.

The water tank on the plane was nearly full, but she was still refuelling. With only one fuel hose, they had had to wait for the Robin before C-SPRY could take her turn. Now they were back to business.

"Here's your target. Bit of an odd one – the hydrant network the firemen were using has been cut off and they need supplies. There's a dirt track racing circuit here at Northside. Can you land on it?" Rose pointed at the large-scale map, and Jim examined it closely.

"Unless anything's really changed since the map was printed, yeah. Have to be that long straight though, and west to east or there won't be space to turn her round and take off."

"Good. Plan is that the guys up there will hook in, drain your water tank and then you get out. They can use the water more effectively than you. Watch out for other sprayers coming in, you aren't the only one on this duty."

"Two thousand litres is nothing to those trucks." Jim shook his head in disbelief.

"It's all more minutes fire-fighting time." She corrected quite bluntly, and Jim nodded.

"Anything else they need?"

"Way ahead of you. Diesel – Matt's carry cans are full. First aid. Jill's done a pack for the seat, and we've thrown in some energy bars and drinking water." Rose paused and he nodded.

"Sounds good. Get it packed and stowed while I check the plane."

Shortly afterwards the crop sprayer bounced down the runway and staggered into the sky. Jim disliked flying the plane when it was this heavily loaded, but did not see much of a choice. He climbed carefully, setting course towards the dirt track and announcing his flight path on the radio in case any other traffic was in the area. The twenty minute journey passed quietly enough as he focused on the radio transmissions trying to hear how Matt was doing. He was almost at his destination when he heard EVAC-24 announce its landing approach at Lakeside and relaxed, switching attention to his approach to Northside.

Northside was the hillside above the town, and as he approached he saw the problem. The race track itself was partway up the hillside, and the town at the base of the hill was evacuating. Between the track and the town a frond of fire had spread through the forest, cutting the two off, and it was growing wider.

Abruptly he changed course, realising the fire would be giving off thermals which would complicate his planned approach. Looping back to avoid flying over the fire itself he lined up on the racetrack.

"C-SPRY 10 on approach," he radioed, aware that Rose had mentioned other traffic flying in.

"FT263 receiving. The track's clear for you." Jim blinked. When he had been told the team was cut off, he had not realised they still had radio. He began his descent, acutely aware of the winds whipping across the hillside, and the gusts of hot air from the fire, and hoped he could avoid the worst of the turbulence. The heavy load gave him a little more stability, as water could not slosh in a full tank, but if something went wrong it gave him less chance to recover.

As he approached the track itself he found a new problem. The warm earth shimmered with its own heat haze as the sun beat down on it, and the thermals from the fire climbed the hillside. Jim cursed. He had hoped to land by the start of the straight stretch, but between the ground effect and the thermals the crop duster was hovering above the runway and refused to touch down. He considered killing the engines and trying to force the aircraft down, but with a sizeable length of the makeshift runway already behind him, he decided against it. With more power to the engines, the crop sprayer picked up speed and lifted away.

"C-SPRY 10 going around," he reported, and then cringed. If it was not embarrassing enough to say when talking about a landing that should have been routine, the crop sprayer's owner was listening on the same channel. When Matt found out why he had gone around, the ribbing would be merciless.

Putting it out of his mind, Jim circled back. This time his approach was slower and more shallow, bleeding off speed as the crop duster was buffeted by gusts. He held course, trying to correct to keep her straight and stable on their approach. As the aeroplane reached the start of the runway, already near stalling speed, Jim took a chance and pushed her down.

As the thermals pushed the wings up the aircraft slid sideways, one back wheel touching, then bouncing. He corrected, trying to make her level out before the crop sprayer could bounce between the front wheels and go out of control. Quickly he cut the engine power, trying to reduce speed as fast as possible, while he raised the nose to change the aircraft's angle. The sudden loss of lift worked and the aircraft's three wheels hit the dirt track again with a teeth-rattling bump and bounce. It bounced again, and then once more for good measure, before it settled and he could bring it to a stop. At some point along the runway he had bitten his cheek, and as the firemen ran up he climbed out gingerly and gestured to the water tank.

The fire engine was driven alongside. He had expected them to connect to the spray somehow, but instead the water intake was opened and a hose swiftly inserted into the tank. The small water gauge on the fire engine's side began to climb as Jim heard the pump activate.

"You alright, mate?" The voice jerked Jim out of his thoughts. With the water transfer now underway, one of the firemen was taking time to check on the pilot. Jim swallowed a mouthful of blood, pointing his fingers at the cockpit of the aircraft and said thickly:

"Suppliesh." The word was choked, and the fireman looked alarmed.

"Rattled your brains on the landing?"

"Noh. Bit my..." Jim couldn't manage the right word and waved his hand at his mouth. The fireman guessed and his face lightened.

"Bit your tongue?" It was close enough, and as Jim nodded gratefully he turned back to the crew. "You two. Supply packs in the aircraft. Get 'em." Guided by Jim's gestures, the fire crew quickly accessed the mechanic's cabin and retrieved the packages. The supplies were rapidly and enthusiastically pillaged and the diesel added to the fire engine's tank. Thoughtfully the empty diesel cans were wiped off, sealed and secured back in the mechanic's cabin. Jim had not realised Rose had included sun block in the emergency pack, but the speed it was shared round and the empty bottle disposed of told him it had been a good choice.

"You keep bringing stuff like this with you, you'll be welcome up here any time," the fireman joked, as the water tank on the aircraft ran dry.

"Will you want another run?" Jim asked, carefully talking around the sore part of his mouth.

"Hopefully this'll be enough." The fireman frowned at the water tank on the fire engine, only a third full.

"What happened to the other two supply planes?" Jim asked, suddenly remembering. He had not heard any other traffic on the radio as he attempted his approach.

"Couldn't land." The fireman wore a slight smirk. Now that one of the supply planes had got through, the failure could be funny.

"Had a few problems myself." Jim chuckled slightly ruefully, feeling his sore cheek where it was beginning to swell. The firemen had finished stowing the hose and the engine was getting ready to drive off. "If that's it, I'll be heading off once you're clear."

He got a nod and a wave from the crew as the engine reversed away and turned down towards the fire. The take off was easier this time. The winds had picked up and the main problem was keeping the plane straight as she accelerated, fighting the gusts that tried to tip her disastrously on a wingtip. Once airborne he climbed steeply, wanting to get away from the thermals and turbulence around the hillside and safely into level flight. Behind him, further down the hill, a white jet of spray lifted skywards and showered down on the flames.

As he landed at Brooke's Vale he noticed the Robin was not back yet, but two figures were crouched by the side of the fuel store. Halting the plane further back to avoid any chance of an accident, he climbed out and walked across.

"Oy! I want words!" One of the figures that straightened up was definitely Rob, brandishing a spanner in one hand. "You let me sleep in!"

"Well, it's not as if you have a plane to fly," Jim replied, as meekly as he could. "And speaking of planes, this one needs fuel and water. So does the pilot."

The reminder of why they were there deflected Rob's ire. The crop sprayer was rolled into position and the fuel and water hoses attached. As the pumps began work, Jim sat down quite suddenly in the dirt.

"You OK?" Rob asked, coming across quickly to check on him. Jim honestly was not sure. His legs were uncomfortably cramped, his lower back ached, and his shoulders were stiff. "The Dromedar's not an aircraft you want to spend a long time in, especially if you aren't used to it."

"Yeah. You were smart, grabbing the Robin to make sure you got a comfortable seat." Flexing his legs, Jim climbed to his feet and tried to ease sore muscles.

"Hey, I wanted to save people from the fire, not piss on it!" Rose and Jim exchanged a glance. Rob's relationship to Matt really showed on occasion.

"Just expresshing my opinion." Jim riposted, having trouble with 'expressing' as his swollen cheek made its effects known. Rob looked at him closely and took an arm to steady him, helping him towards a spare crate.

"Don't tell me. Uncle Matt's plane beat you up."

"Rou' landing. Can you get her refuelled?"

"We've got the other fuel hose working," Rob answered. "Do two planes at a time if you need to. Makes it easier if you get anything else flying from here."

"Where's Matt?" Jim asked. His thoughts were scattered, head full of thermals, ground effect, and aches and pains.

"On his way. He refuelled at the airport to save time. Once he gets back I'll take the rest of the passengers and continue from there." Rob looked better for the sleep, Jim had to admit, and ready to fly. Ironically Jim was now the one who needed rest, and it was painfully obvious to the other two.

"Meanwhile, you will be getting some shut-eye and an ice-pack," Rose ordered, much to Rob's amusement. "It'll take an hour for C-SPRY to fly again, and you're on standby for that racetrack."

"Standby!" Jim exclaimed, struggling to his feet. Rose shrugged.

"You managed to land. The other aircraft ended up soaking the hillside," she said off-handedly. Jim nodded and wandered into the hangar, avoiding the house. If the evacuees from the Rookery were still around he really did not feel like talking to people at the moment. He shook out a couple of Matt's blankets and resting his back against warm metal he went to sleep.

His eyes opened to the sound of raised voices. Quietly he stood up, straining to hear what was going on, and walked up behind one of the hangar's half closed doors to listen.

"I'll pay you alright?" That was Roger Barnhurst's unmistakeable voice, insistent and demanding.

"Look Roger, this isn't about money." Rob, trying to be the voice of reason.

"Really? I'm a local, but you'll fly total strangers out first."

"Checking on your beach hut is not a priority." Matt's voice was calm and unruffled. He must have returned while Jim was asleep. "Why don't you just drive there?"

"Out the front of the valley and round? That's two hours drive. It's twenty minutes in the plane."

"So start driving now." Matt was utterly unmoved. Jim risked peering out, to see a small crowd gathered around the Robin. The second group of evacuees were ready to go, but Roger was standing in front of the aircraft.

"Look, I'm being reasonable," Roger tried. "If you can just take me up there and drop me off at the beach – "

" – and bog down in the sand and be unable to take off again." Rob completed sarcastically. His flight window was disappearing, and so was his patience.

"At least you'd be safe up there," Roger replied with a shrug.

"If you want out you should drive yourself like everyone else. Look, if I'm not needed again I'll drop this group off and come back here to do some air evac runs."

"You'll take me now." Roger's demand was met with a blank wall of faces, closed in flat silent refusal. "Fine. Then no one goes anywhere."

He grabbed the propeller blade nearest him and swung a kick at the Robin's wing. Jim lunged forward, too far away to do anything, at the same time that Matt and Rob moved helplessly to protect the plane, and then there was a sharp crack and Roger was on the floor. The man they had evacuated was on top of him, swinging another punch into his face. They froze.

Matt was the first to throw off the shock. He put a hand on the man's shoulder and pulled him away. The man turned to him sharply, then saw who it was and let himself be led clear. In the silence Roger coughed and sat up. The evacuee was breathing hard, fist still clenched, and as Roger moved he stepped forward to kick out. Matt caught his arm.

"Thanks Pete. That's enough." Matt looked at Rob, who caught Roger by an arm and hauled him away from the plane. One of the teenage evacuees grabbed Roger's other arm and together they dragged him unceremoniously to the other side of the runway and dumped him down.

"You can't do this. You hit me. I'll press charges." There was stunned incredulity in his voice, but also a fair bit of fear.

"Really? We all saw you take a kick at him. I'd call it self-defence." Matt's voice was calm, and he was even smiling slightly.

"But that's…" Roger broke off in sudden realisation

"Jill what did you see?" Matt asked without turning round.

"Roger grabbed Pete's arm and took a kick at him." The woman pronounced from the doorway of the mobile, glowering at Roger.

"Jim?" Matt asked, eyes still fixed on Roger. Jim nodded agreement, face set.

"That's what happened."

"You see. That's how it is." Matt's voice was still utterly, deathly, calm. "Attacking a man who's lost his house, and all his possessions, now that's low." Roger stood up, brushing himself down and made his final mistake. He took a step towards the aircraft, and Matt drew a breath.

"And if you ever show your poxy arse around my fucking aircraft ever again, it'll be the last sodding thing you ever do! Get the fuck off my land now!"

The sudden bellow and uncharacteristic language held the watchers transfixed. Silence fell, and Roger gathered the last shreds of his dignity. With painful progress he limped across to his car and drove off.

As he left the spell broke. Rob turned instantly to the propeller that Roger had grabbed and began careful examination of the propeller blade and wing edge. Matt joined him while Jill brought the first aid pack out and examined Pete's knuckles, which were rapidly bruising. The kick had not connected, but damage to the propeller where Roger had wrenched at it for leverage might ground the aircraft. There was a tense quiet until Matt and Rob had assured themselves the Robin was undamaged.

"She's OK to fly." Rob stood back and looked at Matt, who nodded agreement. He looked to the evacuees. "Thanks for the help Pete. Let's get you lot down to Lakeside. I want the Robin well away from Roger, just in case he gets any other bright ideas."

The mention of the airport was enough to get people moving, and Pete and the remaining evacuees climbed in, assisted by Matt, as Rob completed his walk round. With a wave, Rob closed the cabin and took off, the little aircraft climbing away easily with its lighter load.

"I hadn't realised it was so fragile." Rose commented, a little shaken by the fight.

"Wood and canvas." Jim answered as he slipped an arm round her. "A foot in the wrong place can do a lot of damage. But it's a dream to fly. Now if he tried to kick the Shackleton's wings I'd have let him."

"I don't think he can get his foot up that high." Rose replied dryly, looking up at the wings they could walk completely underneath.

"Wonder why he was so desperate to get to the beach hut?" Jim pondered and Matt shrugged.

215

"By the waterfront. Must be safer." As Jim nodded, Rose laughed.

"Hardly. His beach hut is halfway up the hillside. I'd say it's more because the fire department announced they were going to tear the lot down as a firebreak."

"Must've left something valuable in it." Jim's tone could not have been less sympathetic.

"Only if it's something he doesn't share with his family. He's happy enough to leave them here." Rose snorted cynically but was interrupted as Jill waved across.

"Guys, choose a pilot. You're up."

"The racetrack?" Jim asked, and she nodded. Matt shot him a look as both pilots silently and instantly agreed Jim would fly it. He already knew the terrain, and privately Matt wanted to be here just in case Roger came back. Simultaneously the pair began the, by now well-practiced, routine of checking over the crop sprayer.

"Won't this leave you short of supplies Matt?" Jim asked as he worked. Rose and Jill had obviously been busy while he slept. The aircraft was already fully fuelled, with a full water tank, ready and waiting for this signal.

Matt popped his head up over the side of the plane.

"Nah. These are Col's. He headed over with some of his."

"Nice of him. How'd he know what was going on?" Matt paused, shooting a quick accusing glance at Rose. Jim's girlfriend smirked at him.

"Well, announcing 'No evac yet.' every hour on the hour was getting boring, and we thought people would forget to tune in, so we decided to spice up our broadcasts with a few lines about what you and the Robin were up to. Smile, you're a celebrity." He scowled at her, as she finished stacking the boxes by the plane and walked off to the Shackleton for the next broadcast. The waiting pack of supplies that Rose and Jill had assembled was quickly secured in the mechanic's cabin, and ten minutes later the crop sprayer was climbing into the same sky that the Robin had so recently vanished into.

Matt rubbed his hands clean as he watched his second plane leave, hoping Jim and Rob would take care. With both aircraft safely away there was little for him to do but wait. From inside the house he could hear the

217

emergency radio and, with the TV on and the radio receiver set up, the scale of the fires was becoming apparent. Despite himself his mind flashed back to the family yesterday, and he found himself wondering how many more would be trapped like that, for lack of water and help. Matt knew he would not get any sleep in the hot afternoon, but with nothing to do his thoughts kept cycling back to a small car, a burning road… a sharp pain in his injured hand brought him back to reality and he realised he had clenched his fists. He needed a distraction.

His favourite one was still available, parked by the runway. Although he could not work on the inside with the ladies using it as a radio station, there were still bits he could do. Walking across to the hangar, he fetched another ladder and the platform he used to work on the plane. Carefully setting it up by one wing, he examined the area until he found somewhere to begin. Picking up the pots of rustproof treatment and paint he settled down by the patch of corrosion he had been working on last night and went back to work completing the repair.

He had only been painting a few minutes when the loud roar brought his head up and turned, even as Jill and Rose rushed outside.

"Was that thunder?" Jill asked incredulously. The hill blocked their view of the land beyond the Vale but the clouds, a sickly ash-grey, could still be seen. Matt abandoned his tools and jumped into the car, remembering his manners long enough to open the passenger door for Jill. Rose waved them away.

"I'll stay with the radio. Let me know what's going on OK?" As she turned back to the house, Matt sped off as quickly as the four-wheeler could take them. The same unspoken prayer lay in all their minds. Rain.

They reached the lay-by at the top of the hill in record time, and looked out at the forest before them. The sky directly above them was still blue, although tendrils of grey ash-filled clouds were slowly invading it, but ahead of them a huge greyish cloud filled the sky, casting a shadow over the land. Below it the fires still raged and on its underside, parts of the cloud reflected the orange flickering lights of the fires. There was no sign of rain.

"If it wasn't thunder, what was it?" Jill asked as they scanned the landscape. "It can't have been a plane down."

219

"No. That loud and we'd have passed the wreckage on the way here." Matt was looking back into the valley, trying to see anything that might have caused the noise. This was why he missed it. Jill did not and he heard her cry out.

"Matt, look!" As he looked where she was pointing, at first he could see nothing. Then a small curl of smoke arose, thickening and strengthening into the plume that told him a new fire had started. Under her breath Jill was counting beside him and staring at her watch.

"...thousand twenty-one, thousand twenty-two" The immense roar of the thunder drowned her out and they froze for a second.

"Forty-three seconds. My watch says forty-six."

"About eight miles then." Matt was watching the forest, not sure if he could see the orange glow of the new fire or if he was imagining it. "Too close. Six miles is the danger zone."

"And still no rain." Her voice was disappointed but not defeated.

"No. So we'd better get back to work, and let people know about the lightning." Matt opened the car door more courteously this time, and they headed back to the airstrip.

Jim reached the racetrack quickly, and was relieved to see that here at least the flames had been beaten back. With the line of fire causing the thermals extinguished and now simply a black scar on the hillside, conditions were much better. This time his landing, although shallow and slow, was a lot smoother and he brought the crop sprayer to a halt near the fire engines at the end of the strip. To his surprise there were two engines here this time, and the new arrival was one he had not seen before. Still in forest service livery, the rugged outsized tyres had massive grips, and it looked like nothing so much as a jeep. It was pulled alongside first, and Jim could see it was caked in mud and had obviously been off-road recently. Assisted by the fire crew he knew, the new arrivals had a hose in the aircraft's water tank almost before Jim had climbed out.

"Supplies in the mechanic's cabin like before. Two diesel cans, first aid stuff and some water bottles." Jim said, snagging the arm of the fireman he remembered.

221

"You make a great first impression, mate." One of the new firecrew commented as they started to unload. The two diesel cans were quickly emptied into the larger engine.

"Any fuel for us?" One of the firemen from the forest crew asked, obviously disappointed. Jim had to shrug, as he realised the smaller engine was not a diesel.

"Sorry, not unless you can take avgas," Jim replied, and then froze. "But if you can take petrol, you can."

"That'll work?" The fireman paused suddenly.

"It's higher octane, so you'll get done for emissions, but it'll run fine." Looking at the huge black clouds rising from the fires, Jim did not think emissions would be a concern at the moment. The fire chief obviously agreed.

"Then can we fill up? We don't want to leave you short." There was an urgency in the fireman's tone that decided Jim.

"She's got a six hundred mile range, and she's fully fuelled. Half the tank's spare."

Siphoning fuel from the crop sprayer proved a more complicated affair, and unlike the water the fire truck had no specialised pump to take it on board. Nonetheless, with a bit of ingenuity, a length of rubber hose from the race track stores provided an answer. While they waited for the water tank to fill, and the fuel to top off, the fire chief filled Jim in.

"Should've let you know about the second engine. Sorry the message didn't get through."

"Don't worry, I was just told to bring water up here." Jim waved him off. "You sure you'll have enough?"

"Yeah," the fireman in charge of the off-road engine replied. "We just need to make sure we can get to the lake. Once we're there the hose can get us all the water we need." Through the rising smoke, Jim could hardly see the lake the fireman gestured at, but he nodded anyway. "I'd say you've saved us an hour or so by dropping in here. Otherwise we'd have been heading all the way down the hill."

"That's enough." As the water pump cut out, the tank full, the crew chief brought an end to the conversation. Once the hose and makeshift siphon were detached, the large engine drove up as the smaller truck pulled away. They did not pause to say goodbye, just headed back to the fire front, turning sharply outside the racetrack. The huge tyres kicked up a cloud of dust from the dry surface as they headed off across the hillside towards the flames.

"Can you do medevac?" The remaining crew chief did not waste words. His crew were already busy linking the water connections to the larger engine, and stowing the supplies in their cab. Jim paused warily. He had flown casualties before, but in military transports with medical staff. The crop sprayer was an entirely different proposition.

"What's the problem?" he asked, considering the issue.

"One of my crew. Broken arm and burns. His breathing gear's been smashed. Can you get him to a hospital?"

"Surely the air ambulance would be better?" Jim's natural caution took hold. Flying a casualty was always a risk, and the crop sprayer was not really equipped for mercy flights.

"He's conscious and walking, so he's not a priority case for the chopper, but while he's up here he's also a concern and distraction for the crew." There was a pause as Jim considered the situation. Refusing and leaving the casualty here would be the sensible option, but he was up here to provide them with any assistance he could. A simple flight out should not be a problem.

"Where do you need him taken?" Jim took a quick look at his watch. This late in the day, they would never get the water tank refilled for an extra flight in the crop sprayer. If an air ambulance didn't get up here in the next hour the casualty would be stranded here through the night with untreated injuries. And Jim knew the decision he would want the pilot to make in this situation if Jake were the one injured.

"Lakeside would be best. They've got the medical facilities to cope."

"I can drop him at Lakeside airport," Jim replied. "But understand, I've got no medical training if anything goes wrong."

"Understood." The crew chief nodded, then walked across to the engine and knocked on the cab door. "Tell base C-SPRY 10 is taking Paul into Lakeside for medical treatment. Paul, get out here."

"I'll manage, chief." Looking at the young man who had climbed out, his arm in a makeshift sling and soot-covered face the picture of determination, Jim had to say he disagreed.

"I don't care. I'd rather be a man down than have a man down. Now get in the plane." The crew chief's words were harsh, but his concern was obvious. Jim gestured the fireman across to the rear-facing seat and helped him into the mechanic's position. With the man's left arm unusable, it was surprisingly difficult, and Jim had to secure the belts.

"It'll be a rough take off on this surface," he warned and the fire fighter, Paul, looked down at his arm.

"It's splinted," he said stoically.

"OK. Then get the headset on. I'm trained to worry when casualties go silent." With a bit of fiddling to avoid the worst of the burns it was settled in place. Jim paused, already having second thoughts as he realised the extent of the man's injuries, but it was too late to back out now.

"Water tank's empty." The shout from beside the crop sprayer let Jim know the fire engine was getting ready to leave. With practiced ease the hose was detached and the engine pulled back. With the passenger settled and the fire engine moving away, Jim did a walk round to ensure everything was intact after all the activity around the fuel tank, before he climbed in himself. His passenger was very pale, virtually huddled in his seat clutching his damaged arm, and staring out of the window at the rising smoke. Jim let him watch the fires, knowing the fire fighter was not in a state to chat. He had seen that reaction in the injured before, taking themselves away from the source of the pain. If the fire fighter had untreated burns, he must be in agony. He could not bring himself to ask what had happened, but from the twigs and dirt smeared on the fireman's uniform, Jim suspected a tree had fallen on him.

With the fire engine clear of the plane, he turned the crop duster, lining it up for the take off. The rough dirt track was going to be hell on the fire fighter's arm. All he could do was make the run as quick and smooth as possible. Grimacing he increased the throttle and the aircraft accelerated, lurching on the bumpy ground. There was a hiss of pain from behind him as the plane jolted, and then it reached take off speed and Jim rotated to lift away. In his concern for the passenger he was almost too early, and the aircraft rocked in the air before entering the smooth shallow climb he wanted. As he turned for Lakeside, entering level flight, he saw the small shape of the fire engine pulling out of the racetrack behind them and silently wished them luck. Then he thumbed the radio.

"C-SPRY 10 to Base, taking a casualty to Lakeside. Request a route around the fires to avoid known turbulence." The acknowledgement was almost instant, and he realised the fire crew must have sent the details ahead while they were fuelling. As he turned to skirt the fire zone and reach the airport, he knew he would need to avoid turbulence where possible. With both pilot and passenger strapped in it was not the threat it had been on the frantic flight from the Rookery, but the last thing his passenger needed was a bumpy ride. Privately Jim admitted to himself that he could do with some easy flying after the events of the past few days.

As Control came back with the bearings for his route, one hand dropped automatically to the trim control for one of the swift automatic adjustments that were becoming second nature. His legs and arms complained that the damage from his heavy handed flying had already been done and, even with his mid-day nap, Jim was exhausted.

"You alright back there?" he asked, belatedly remembering he had a passenger to worry about.

"Yeah." The fire fighter sounded as tired as Jim felt, and with better cause. "Thanks." The word was added quickly as an afterthought.

The journey was mercifully short, broken only by Jim's regular checks that his passenger was still conscious. Between his own exhaustion and the firefighter's injuries, neither of them were up to conversation and the smoke plumes billowing from the forest below stood in shocking testament to the scale of the devastation. Fortunately it was only twenty minutes before the awkward, uncomfortable, journey was over and they were asking permission to land.

The Lakeside's business airport had been turned into the base of operations for the area. Two large fire fighting aircraft were refuelling, dwarfing the light aircraft that usually flew out. On the car park, a series of large mobile buildings had been constructed, one with a red cross at the front. Beyond them, in the field, the helicopters were using the flat grass as their base of operations. This close to sundown there was a controlled urgency to it, the firefighters trying to get one more run in, supplies being hastily dispatched to those out in the field overnight, and makeshift medevac flights like his own trying to get casualties in and then back to their own bases before the dark grounded them for the night.

Jim took a breath and concentrated. In airspace this crowded pilots were always only one mistake away from a collision, and he had to trust the tower to guide him in. He joined the stack behind a larger crop sprayer, C-SPRY 4 as the radio told him. As he turned the crop sprayer, keeping his place, Jim glanced below them to see two more aircraft queuing on the taxiway, waiting for their turn to take off. The runway had been put into mixed use, aircraft taking off and landing from the same runway. As long as all the aircraft kept moving in the same direction it would work, and allowed more aircraft to use the runway than normal. It just required a little more focus from the pilots.

In front of them, C-SPRY 4 received permission to land and began its approach run. As it landed and taxied off the end of the runway, on the ground below Jim saw a Canadair began its take-off run. As it lifted away, it was Jim's turn.

With mixed use, there was no leeway for a go-around. If he needed to pull up, he would have to circle sharply away to clear the airspace and then rejoin the stack before he could get another chance to land. Despite his fatigue he needed to get this one right first time. He blinked to clear his gaze, reassuring himself that with a mild, steady headwind, no thermals or gusts to complicate matters, this should be utterly routine. Grateful for his passenger's silence, he came out of his final turn lined up on the runway and committed himself to the approach.

His aircraft was lighter than most, and made a textbook touchdown in a short distance. Even as he let out a relieved breath, he was being directed to leave the runway at a midpoint exit halfway down to clear the space. As he turned onto the assigned exit, another of the large fire fighting aircraft swung into position behind him at the start of the runway, spooling up for its own take-off run and one final flight before dark. In the bustle of the airport, it was all Jim could do to follow the tower's directions to taxi to their assigned bay, swinging onto the grass field and out of the chaos for a brief moment.

Gratefully he shut the engine off and let his head loll back. It was surprising how much the short trips had taken out of him. The next thing he heard was the aircraft doors being opened, and he sat up quickly as his passenger was helped out. He watched as Paul was loaded into a small airport runabout, but then had to assure a concerned medic that there was nothing wrong with him personally, that he was just the delivery pilot. As the medical crew drove away, he was surprised to be signalled almost immediately by the Tower, requesting that he notify them when ready to proceed as they needed the bay.

With a deep breath to steady his nerves, Jim composed himself and acknowledged, starting the engines and swinging back into the melee, joining the queue of other aircraft at the start of the runway, while above them the stack waiting to land turned slowly. How Rob had stood doing this constantly for two days, he really could not imagine. All he wanted now was to go home.

It was almost dark by the time he got back, and he was surprised at how quickly the day had gone. All Jim really wanted now was food and bed, and as he moved the crop sprayer into her assigned space and turned off the engine in the gathering dusk it was all he was thinking of. The transmission as his radio crackled into life surprised him.

"C-SPRY 10 are you clear of the runway?" He could have sworn that that was Rose's voice on the regional frequency, and then belatedly remembered the Shackleton.

"Yes, I'm parked in her bay," he replied, aware he was breaking protocol but too tired to care.

"Good. Stay there. F407, you are cleared to land."

"F407 to Brooke's Vale Tower. Acknowledged." That was a voice he didn't know, and as Jim twisted in his seat to look along the runway he heard the faint sound of an aircraft, rapidly growing louder. A speck of light in the gathering gloom expanded, taking on the familiar form of an aeroplane. Matt walked out of the hangar and wandered across, nodding a greeting as he stepped up on the wing and leant against the window.

"We've got guests for tonight," the older pilot explained.

"What happened?"

"Human error." Matt smiled wryly. "They don't have time to get back to Lakeside until well after dark."

"And with all the ash up there it's too dangerous to try." Jim nodded, and then was drowned out as the aircraft came in to land. It was a rough affair, the pilot perhaps too eager or exhausted to manage anything better, but then the aircraft was down and stopped.

The new arrival was in a sorry state, ash marking her wings and grass stains on the underside telling of take-off in long vegetation. Under the smears however, the gleam of yellow paint was visible and the silhouette, sitting next to the crop sprayer, was unmistakeable. Jim started to chuckle and then laugh.

"No wonder you're so happy to have them."

"What, because they fly the fire fighting version of our Seaspray?" Matt tapped the crop duster's side affectionately. "I said yes because they know the plane and so do we. I wouldn't leave anyone stranded out there."

The front door had opened, and the pilot stepped out carefully. In much the same shape as his plane he stumbled, leaning on the fuselage, while behind him another crewman began to extricate himself. Matt went across to help, but when Jim climbed out of his own cockpit and tried to follow he found his own knees buckling. Matt stopped and surveyed them, and then nodded decisively.

"Inside. Food. Shower. Beds. You three need it."

Day Three

Next morning with five minutes to sunrise, Matt was completing his walk round on the crop duster. Beyond him, already in position on the runway, the yellow shape of the fire fighter almost gleamed. Once the pilots had gone to sleep, Rose, Jill and Matt had gone to work, refuelling and in Matt's case repairing both aircraft. He had been certified to maintain the type for years. They had left the fire fighting system strictly alone, uncertain whether it took chemicals or water, but once he had finished Rose and Jill had set to work with wax and polish. They knew their work would be quickly dirtied, but also that it was one way to show their appreciation for the crew's efforts.

The news overnight had not been good. As the wind pushed the huge cloud away from the fire, the lightning that struck beneath it was starting new blazes in areas previously unaffected. Now day was breaking and the fire fighting aircraft were returning to the fray, all they could do was see how much of their work had been undone, and try to make up the ground they had lost.

As he settled into the cockpit, Matt heard the fire fighter confirming his take off run, and saw the yellow aircraft begin to move. They were off to Lakeside for a refill of foam. C-SPRY 10 had his own assignment: The small village of Lowry, now directly in the fire's path. After the failure of their aerial appliance, the long ladder that would normally let them soak down the roofs, Lowry Fire Department had made a most unusual request. It was far from standard practice, and it would tax his skill as a crop sprayer, but if Matt could help, he would. He was just glad his tank had been thoroughly cleaned.

While the fire crews on the ground would work on diverting the front itself, his mission was simpler. Some of the villagers had stayed behind to try to save the town, but there was far too much for them to soak on their own and if a fire started from floating ash it would be hard to put out. His two thousand litre load, air dropped, could change that.

As the other aircraft turned for Lakeside and cleared his airspace, Matt began his own run. Jim was still asleep, apparently exhausted, although he had done the majority of the flying yesterday and Matt could not begrudge him the rest. As the crop sprayer lifted away, he entered level flight and then turned sharply towards the village. He tried to put his disquiet to one side, but nagging doubts kept resurfacing. The fire should never have reached Lowry, unless it had jumped the firebreaks. It was an uncomfortable thought. Idly he flexed his damaged hand, feeling the pain through it but knowing he had use of the fingers. Doubts aside, he had his own piece of flying to do.

As he looked around for landmarks, the smoke from the fire front grew thicker. He reduced height to four hundred feet, hoping the worst of it would pass above him, carried on the wind. Visibility was poor, but beneath him he could make out the road to the village and followed it. He was flying directly into the wind now, and smoke and ash stung his eyes. Thankfully he spotted the church spire ahead beneath him and banked to bring himself into line for his first pass.

Far higher than he would be for crop spraying, Matt knew he had to correct for wind speed and direction, or the spray would simply be carried away. With the strong wind blowing directly towards the town that left him making his first run between the town and the fire front to make sure the town was soaked. As he circled once more he checked the height of the rooftops and nodded to himself. The trees outside the town made low flying difficult, but it was possible if he got the angle right. He was about to break every rule in the book about flight height over inhabited areas, but somehow he did not think the residents would complain.

He came in at two hundred feet above the forest as slow as he dared, and then dropped the crop sprayer into a shallow dive as he hit the spray. Behind him the water became a white cloud, falling on the town. He could not see exact distances behind him but a sharp banking turn over the town's outskirts, still spraying, brought him back alongside his initial pass. To his relief he had judged correctly. The roofs and paved roads glistened wetly as the water settled on the surfaces. Staying as low as he dared, to make sure as much of the spray reached the town as possible, he swung round in another turn for his next parallel pass. If nature would not give them rain, he'd make his own.

The initial passes complete, he performed a slow circuit, spraying the outside houses once more. He was low enough to catch a glimpse of one of the residents waving to him from a balcony, bucket full of water by his side. The people who had stayed here were ready to play their part in defending their homes.

Water tank empty, Matt finished the circuit and lifted away towards Brooke's Vale. Absently he let the base know where he was going, but his mind was elsewhere. Lowry had natural firebreaks around it, and should never have been under threat. Nature's capricious trick with the wind and lightning had brought the fire where it usually would not be. In the last three days, the winds had not changed. Blowing from the inland constantly, they were driving the flames towards Brooke's Vale. Ahead of the fire, the huge pyro-cumulous cloud it had generated advanced steadily, bringing the lightning and hot ash that let the fire jump all the painstakingly prepared defences. If the winds did not change, then for the first time in memory Brooke's Vale would burn.

Matt was not the only one to wonder. Jim was watching the airstrip's windsock in concern. The forecast did not indicate any change in the wind in the near future. The ominous cloud filled half the sky and as he watched he fancied it moving inexorably towards them. He did not like the way his thoughts were turning.

"Rose, what do you think of that?" Rose looked round from where she had climbed out of the Shackleton after giving the latest update. She looked up and shuddered.

"Scary," she said, with heavy understatement, and then stopped. "Jim, I know this will sound silly but –" She broke off. Jim looked at her wondering if they had the same thought.

"Go on." There was no mockery in his tone, and she swallowed and voiced the unthinkable.

"I know there's been no evacuation signal, and Brooke's Vale has never burned, but despite that, should we start evacuating the vulnerable?"

"I don't know," Jim admitted, torn between taking the safe route and not wanting to start a panic. Then he added his own blunt truth. "If the wind doesn't change, that fire is coming here."

"I'll let people know. If they start moving now there's plenty of time to get out." Rose was suddenly back to her decisive self, heading for the Shackleton. Jim only just caught her parting words "If they believe me."

Matt's crop duster appeared in the sky, landing and taxiing to its usual position. Only Jim was waiting for him. As Jim connected the water and fuel, Matt climbed out and threw him an indecipherable look.

"They're trying to hold the fire outside Lowry," he said. Jim finished the connections and stood up.

"It's jumped the firebreaks. We think it might reach here. Rose's getting the word out." He expected Matt to laugh, and hoped he would. Instead he got an abrupt nod.

243

"Very good idea." Matt's solid agreement made Jim's fears seem uncomfortably real.

"Could we spray down the valley?" Jim asked.

"Just done a town. The tank barely made it. Houses here are too widely spaced. I need a drink." He headed into the hangar, ignoring the coffee and heading straight for the beer. Jim watched him, amused when Matt automatically looked up at where the Shackleton's wing should be and humphed before he wandered outside. By the time Jim caught up, surely enough, Matt was standing under one wing, examining it closely.

"Too bad she doesn't fly. That's an awful lot of water you could be dropping," Jim quipped, and then caught sight of Matt's face as the pilot froze. He rushed to cover his gaffe. "Or you could just park her at the valley entrance with concrete on the wings and blow the fire back."

"Right up until the Taverners complain that the noise spooks their horses." Matt had unbent a little with the alcohol and Jim joined him in a chuckle.

244

"And then Roger will demand the eyesore be moved," Jim added.

"No, Roger will demand we fly it to his beach hut with only him on board," Matt corrected, and then paused. "Actually I was just going to sit in her."

"What?"

"If the fire gets here. She's got more welds than rivets, with a metal hangar on cleared scrubland. Not much short of a firestorm's going to damage her."

"You know I hadn't thought of that." Jim blinked, considering it. He had to admit Matt's plan sounded good, although he was not sure whether the aircraft was proof against smoke. The noise of engines on the road disturbed him, and he took a look outside.

"Hey, Matt."

"Hay is for horses."

"Odd you should say that. The Taverners just showed up." As Matt turned in surprise, he saw that Jim was right. There were four cars in the little convoy, two towing horseboxes out of which the animals stared bemused. As they parked, the two pilots walked down to meet them, as Jill came out of the house and waved to the cars. She was deep in

245

conversation by the time they got there. Vic Taverner turned to Matt as they walked up.

"So what's the best way out?" He grinned. "You seem to be the ones with the connections."

"Go out of the valley, turn right and take the main road all the way up to the junction by Coomb. Then turn left and head for the Moorlands hotel. They've been told to expect people and it's all under evacuation rules."

"What, nowhere closer?" Vic frowned.

"They're holding the fire just outside Lowry," Matt stated bluntly, and the two visitors went pale.

"That close? Then why – we thought we'd better leave when we heard your signal because of the horses and the guests. Where's the official notice?"

"Brooke's Vale never burns," Jill said quietly.

"There's a first time for everything." Mary Taverner didn't think much of that argument. "We need to get moving. What about you?"

"Cram four in the crop duster and fly out. We've got a while yet," Jim answered. Satisfied, the visitors said their goodbyes and drove off. Rose climbed out of the Shackleton and came to join them, shaking her head to clear it.

"Taking a break from the radio," she said, rubbing an ear.

"Think they'll be OK?" Matt asked, looking at the receding cars.

"The route I gave them keeps them away from the fire and off the blocked roads. As long as they follow it they will be fine. The Moorland's expecting guests, so that's not a problem," Jill replied.

"How did you swing that?" Jim asked. The Moorlands was not a cheap hotel, being the kind of upper class locale that had space for a guest to put horses or helicopters, and enough connections to keep it off the evacuation plans. Jill nodded at Rose, who grinned.

"Gran knows the owner. Well, to be honest she knows the owner's mother, so it all works out the same." She chuckled slightly and then sobered. "Seriously, how do we get out?"

"I'm not sure," Jim replied. "Once we leave here, C-SPRY 10 goes out of operation and so does Radio Shackleton. All the local airports are closed or overloaded."

"I'd like to leave it as late as possible," Jill admitted, pausing to listen as another vehicle went down the road out of the valley. "That was the Royces. It looks like some people listened."

"The ones with kids and animals," Matt said. "If we're right, you two will have saved a few lives yourselves."

"And if we're wrong, we've panicked everyone for no good reason," Rose remarked cynically. "Our evacuation plan?"

"This is scrubland and grass up here. Doesn't burn well. We can fly out in the crop duster. You're all adults. You can keep still," Matt looked at the cropsprayer and frowned. It was going to be a very tight fit.

"Better squeezed than seared huh?" Rose said, and then squealed. "Jim! Put me down!"

"I thought you wanted to be squeezed," he protested, grinning at her as she kicked playfully. The words were light, but the tone behind them carried a serious edge. Matt smiled and wandered back to the Shackleton to give them some privacy. Jill had vanished back to the radio in the office, obviously with the same idea.

More cars passed on the road on the way out before the crop duster was refuelled, and

Matt amused himself by counting off the residents as they left. The Wainwrights, with Granny in the car asleep and snoring no doubt. The Mistry clan went past in three cars, the older parents and then the grown children and families with their large dogs panting in the trailer behind them. There were a few he did not recognise, softened by distance or hard to see in the ash-filled air.

Ready for the next run, Matt began to check the crop sprayer over, while Rose vanished inside to get their next mission. Instead of Rose, it was a white-faced Jill who emerged.

"It's official. We just got the evacuation signal." She bent over to catch her breath as Matt and Jim exchanged stunned glances. Rose ran past them for the Shackleton and climbed up. In the silence they could hear her quite clearly.

"This is Radio Shackleton. The official evacuation signal has been given. Leave now. Do not wait or …"

Outside Matt recovered first.

"I'll take the sprayer up and hose down the exit road. Need to keep it open as long as we can," he said, going to the pilot's door.

"Fine. I'll get things ready here. Set up a few firebreaks on the hill." Jim paused. "They've left this very late. Let's hope we have time."

"Rose will be passing on the info to anyone who might not know." Jill recovered her breath. "The main danger is the road by the valley, about four miles outside. The fire front is closing on it."

"Then I'm off." Matt shut the door and began to prepare for take off. Jill ran back to the house to monitor the emergency channels, while Jim vanished into the hangar. Another car passed on the road outside and then another, obviously already underway when the signal was sent.

Matt took off, following the road out. He knew the danger point well, the bend in the road outside where one fork headed to Lowry. The other bent back round the base of the hills whose other side formed one of the cliffs that bounded Brooke's Vale and then led north to the coast and safety. With the northern cliff trails impassable to vehicles, the bottleneck at the valley entrance, and fire closing in, it was the only route out still open.

He stayed low, above the treetops, quickly overtaking the cars as he followed the line of the road, looking through the smoke for the orange flicker that would tell him where the fire was. Where Lowry had been all he could see was smoke rising, and the acrid smell in the air was overwhelming. He reached the bend in minutes and looked down. The fire front was still miles away, but if the winds remained strong and the fire broke through the defences it could cross that distance in minutes. Above him the clouds churned, filled with smoke and ash, bringing the twin threats of turbulence and lightning into play.

Matt was reluctant to spray the road itself, afraid that water would mix with the ash on its surface, turning it into slick mud. Instead he banked towards the forest and began quick short sprays, hoping to take the hot ash out of the air before it could start a blaze by the road. As he traversed back and forth he saw first one car, then the next, make it round the curve and out onto the road to safety.

As the third car approached, the smoke grew thicker. Matt looked round uncertainly and then saw the cause and thumbed the radio.

"This is C-SPRY 10 in Map Square A4. There appears to be a smoke plume three miles west of the crook on the main road. Can you confirm?" He had never been good at giving directions, and there was a pause that seemed to last minutes while he circled.

"New plume confirmed C-SPRY 10. No crews available."

"C-SPRY 10. I've half a tank left. Commencing spray." He did not think twice. While the tank may have limited effect on established fires, hopefully he could damp this one down before it truly took hold. It was too close to the road for his comfort, regardless.

His first pass took him directly over the smoke, leaving a cloud of white water vapour behind him, condensing and falling. Without waiting he turned, a second pass leaving another cloud as close to the treetops as he dared and the smoke beneath him intensified. He completed a third run, wondering if the water was even making it through the thick canopy of leaves to the fire in the undergrowth below. A fourth pass, and the water had soaked the leaves and treetops, but the smoke plume still rose, growing denser. For a moment, his hand hovered over the water dump, but then he pulled it back. Emptying the tank in one stream might put the fire out, but if he missed he would not get another chance and the dump was not designed for accuracy. His fifth pass, and the spray from his last run settled on the windscreen, droplets running down and carving rivulets through the ash. The crop duster could not turn tightly enough to circle above the fire and spray continuously and he pulled away frustrated. The smoke plume still rose steadily.

He climbed, then turned the aircraft into a diving turn, curving over the fire to release as large a targeted spray as he could. Behind him as he pulled up a cloud rose, grey smoke and white steam combined. He turned the crop sprayer away to avoid being scalded. The wind carried the cloud away quickly, and he came in again, diving and banking to target the seventh pass as best he could. A second cloud, less than the first, arose. He brought the crop sprayer around again and began to hope. He could no longer see the smoke, but he completed the eighth pass anyway, and pulled up.

"C-SPRY 10 to base. It's had five hundred litres on it and I can't see smoke anymore. Returning to the road." Exhausted, Matt hardly heard the response as he swung back. A quarter of a tank left, he still needed to make sure the road stayed open as long as he could.

As he returned he caught sight of another truck retreating, this one towing a trailer as another family made their way out. The Williams, with their wheelchair bound grandfather, had obviously decided not to take the chance of staying. Matt turned back and hit the spray, hoping others had made it out while he was occupied with the new plume. Pass complete, he ended the spray and banked back towards the road.

The cabin filled with white light, and a massive roar filled the aircraft. The crop sprayer rocked, caught in a massive wave of turbulence. Temporarily blinded, Matt blinked frantically, throwing the aircraft into a climb trying to get clear of the trees so he could level out. As the awful roar of the thunder passed, the turbulence lessened. He let the crop sprayer fly straight, trying to clear the black spots and after images that obscured his vision. For a moment he thought the plane had been struck, but it was flying well, and the controls were not affected. He looked round, trying to get his bearings and see if there was any visible damage to the aircraft. Above him the huge cloud rolled and boiled. Driven by the wind, stubbornly refusing to yield the rain they needed, the lightning that came with it allowed the fire to jump ahead of the fire front. Ash and smoke filled the cabin and Matt coughed as he turned the plane back towards the vale. That was when, through the gloom, the flickering orange light caught his eye.

He turned away from the valley, following the road that curved around its side. On the hillside above the last safe road out of Brooke's Vale, the lightning stroke had started a fire that had quickly taken hold. He stared in horrified fascination, knowing that the hills, while impassable to vehicles, were covered in thick vegetation. The fire could climb it in moments.

Matt lined up carefully, knowing that what remained in his water tank would have little effect, but determined to try anyway. He hit transmit again.

"C-SPRY 10 to base. New fire front north-west-west of Brooke's Vale, less than half a mile from the road." He hit the spray, turning and circling. Clouds of steam rose, but through it the flames reflected orange and red. Matt pulled away, turning to let the cloud disperse before he tried another run. As he did so, he saw they had already lost.

The lightning strike had not just set the tree it struck on fire, it had brought it down blazing. Loosely anchored in the scrubby soil the tree had tumbled, taking others and spreading the fire with it, until the pile of burning debris reached the bottom of the hill, and the road. He did not bother contacting Brooke's Vale, knowing Rose and Jill were monitoring the emergency channel anyway.

"C-SPRY 10 to Emergency Services. The road out of Brooke's Vale is completely blocked. Fire and fallen trees after a lightning strike. Map segment –" he spared a glance. "B3."

There was no point trying to fight that fire. Instead he turned back along the road, praying that Rose and Jill would find a way to get the word out.

To Matt's shock, a blue transit rounded the curve ahead of him. Bill Jones was an old friend, and always careful on the road. He was doing less than fifty on the escape route, and Matt swallowed, wondering how to signal him. To make matters worse, Bill had seen the plane, and a hand reached out of the passenger window and waved. For a moment, Matt was back fighting the fire on the road by the gorge, trying to save the family by the road bridge. He was not going to fail again.

The crop duster pulled round in a tight circle as he pulled ahead of the car. He descended to near treetop height as he turned back, racing over them, frantically waggling the aircraft's wings. He could only hope they would realise it was a warning, not a greeting. Behind him, Bill's van slowed as Matt pulled the crop duster into another tight turn, ready to repeat the manoeuvre. The blue van had come to the bottom of the incline leading up towards the blocked road, and abruptly stopped. To Matt's relief the van turned round.

Bill must have seen something that scared him, because he put his foot down on the way back. Behind them, the road was blocked by fire, while ahead of them another fire front was scant minutes from the road, and ash was swirling in the air. Matt pulled the crop sprayer into a low pass, flying repeatedly down the narrowing strip between the road and the fire. Ahead of him, on the road, he could see the sleek green Corvette belonging to the Sampsons. He tried waggling his wings, but through the smoke and ash they had not seen the plane. Matt turned to line up for a low pass, only to see the

Corvette come to a skid stop as the blue transit approached. The van stopped briefly, as the drivers exchanged words, and then it was off. The Corvette turned round on the road, and followed it.

As the two cars began their frantic race towards the vale, Matt swept alongside. Flying low behind the fire, spray on, he had to trust to the wind to carry the water onto the flames, praying it could slow it down enough for the cars to get through. As he outpaced them he swung back, flying over the road, circling again and again, to try to keep the route clear. It was not until the two were safely over the hill and heading back into Brooke's Vale that he peeled off, emptying the last of the water over the flames and then headed for the airfield to land.

To his surprise the airfield was packed. As he landed and pulled in to refuel, he counted at least five cars, and families by them. By the entrance a large white sheet flapped in the breeze, marked with Jill's distinctive scrawl and Rose appeared to be trying to explain what was going on to the increasingly worried crowd. Matt climbed out and took a moment to recover. Then, on reflex, he connected the fuel and water to the little aircraft, and walked down to join the crowd.

"It was a stay or go signal," Rose said patiently. "Either stay in your houses and prepare to fight the fire, or evacuate."

"What about the kids? They can't stay." Maria gestured to her car, where the children watched from the back seat. She was not the only one.

"If we can't get out, our best chance is to choose a house and make a stand there together," Dan said thoughtfully.

"What, like your house, while the rest of ours burn?"

"Shut up, Roger." Even the even-tempered Dan had his limits. It seemed Roger had annoyed more than just the pilots, but as he opened his mouth to lay into Dan, Roger caught sight of Matt's glare. He turned pale and shut up.

"He was trying to get us to fly him to safety earlier, without his family," Rose added calmly, and abruptly anyone who had supported Roger's point of view decided not to mention it. There were a few looks of disgust thrown his way. "Now, the road is blocked, so we need to decide if we stand and fight, or find another way out."

"There's got to be another way out. Why don't we climb for the cliffs and head for the coast?" Colin Marchmont's suggestion was not unexpected coming from the hiker.

"Because the cliffs are covered in greenery, and the fire can climb them faster than you. There aren't any vehicles in town that can make it up the cliff trails, except maybe the western side and that's on fire. Feel free to try it. Just leave the kids behind, they don't need to fry with their parents." Matt had had enough of this, and his answer was decidedly aggressive.

"We're staying." Julia Stilson's quiet voice cut in before things could degenerate further. Her husband was standing close by her, their hands intertwined.

"You can't be serious!" Rose's comment echoed what many were thinking.

"We've got a pool, plenty of water," Mike answered firmly. "It's as good a place to make a stand as any."

"Jake said that if the fire reached us, it would turn into a firestorm. Something to do with the shape of the valley and volatile gases." Rose shifted uncomfortably as the gazes on her turned to frank disbelief. Colin came to her rescue.

"Yeah. He said the same to me. If the valley goes up, no one in it is getting out alive."

"You can't say things like that around the children!" One of the women protested, grabbing her son's arm and trying to push him to the car. The boy resisted, trying to keep following the discussion.

"Lindi, for chrissakes they're teenagers. They have to grow up sometime." Her husband's outburst stunned her into silence, and her son pulled free, taking a few steps away to prevent his mother grabbing him again. The husband nodded to Colin and Rose. "What else did he say?"

"That the valley was dangerous because there was only one way in or out, and if that was blocked you were trapped," Colin began.

"Unless you could fly," Rose finished for him.

"Well, that's you alright then, isn't it?" There was a dangerous pause, as the joke fell flat.

The sound of engines cut through the discussion as a green Corvette veered off the main road and tore up towards the airfield. As it

261

approached, tyres squealing, the crowd shifted slightly, ready to run if it did not stop. Kicking up a dust cloud behind it, wheels slipping on the dirt surface, the car swung sideways and stopped suddenly.

The green sides were streaked with soot, and its soft top marked with smouldering holes and ash. The windscreen wipers had cleared enough for the driver to see, but the rest of the glass was covered with a thick greyish paste. Claude Sampson jumped out of the driver's seat and stopped, briefly staring at the crowd. Then he saw the person he was looking for and dismissed the rest with a shrug.

"Matt, just wanted to say thanks." Claude's tone was off-hand.

"No problem." Matt shrugged it off with a nod. The observers paused confused, expecting an explanation. However, the discussion between one of the most arrogant men in Brooke's Vale and one of the most taciturn appeared to have ended, and no one really wanted to ask.

A second engine could be heard labouring up the road to the airfield. The blue transit parked carefully, next to the Corvette. As the door opened, Bill Jones climbed out and then the portly retiree doubled over trying to get his breath back.

"Doctor!" Claude's call was an order, and the doctor hurried across to check Bill over. Behind him the door of the van opened and frightened faces peered out.

"What Bill is trying to say is that the road from Brooke's Vale is blocked and on fire," Claude added, as the other man wheezed. Bill nodded gratefully and stopped trying to talk as the doctor checked his pulse. "So we need to find a way out. Official evacuation?"

"Overstretched." Rose shook her head. "Jim tried an alternative, but we're probably on our own. Jim?" He shook his head.

"I tried to contact base. I've asked them to send something to get us out, but all the phones are out and the emergency services say it will take time to relay a message. The Shack's transmitter is powerful, but I can't get through to them directly."

"If they could get a couple of troop carrying helicopters up here we could be out in minutes," Roger muttered.

"I've made the request, but they probably can't get here in time. Distance and turbulence," Jim stated flatly. It was the option he preferred, but it was not going to happen.

"So if we're going to get out, we'll have to get ourselves out." Rose shook her head frustrated.

"Matt could fly us out in the crop sprayer." Nick suggested.

"Two at a time. It's an hour round trip to Lakeside or the coast, and the fire will be here before we've finished the second." Rose's comment ended that discussion.

"Can you think of a vehicle that can get forty people out of Brooke's Vale?" Claude asked directly.

Jim paused. His eyes strayed across the valley to the shape beside Matt's barn. Slowly a few more eyes followed his.

"But that can't fly," Roger protested.

"Doesn't have to." Nick, the retired trucker spoke up. "She's reinforced. If we run her at full speed she can bull her way through the fire." The comment brought a shake of the head from Matt, but Jim gave him a sharp glare before he could speak.

"Bulling her way through might not work – spilled aviation fuel would just make things worse," Jim said. "She doesn't have to fly, just make a short hop over the fire. Does it matter how damaged she gets landing if we're in one piece?"

"This is crazy. Why can't we hold it at the valley entrance? With Jake's water tender and the crop sprayer, we could just saturate the entrance so it can't catch." Dan's question was born of honest confusion. Jim took a breath, trying to phrase an answer about the time it took to refill both, how the fire could jump a soaked area, the risk of lightning strikes, and the impossibility of holding it off.

"So we can all be killed when the fire comes over the south ridge and into the valley that way," Rose said bluntly, and Jim closed his mouth.

"What's that noise?" Lindi cut in before they could continue. There was a pause and a sudden hush as people listened.

"Is that an engine?" Colin asked, and a few faces lit up with sudden hope.

"Sounds like a train," Dan said, uncertainly. "In the distance, but still –"

"It's the fire." Jim had heard that sound before at Rookery Lodge. "If we can hear it like that it's close."

While Claude and Bill agreed with Jim, Matt cocked his head slightly and listened. Always before he had been in an aircraft, and the noise of the engines and his radio headphones muffled it. Now he could actually hear the inferno behind the hill and his blood ran cold. The frozen pause gave way to an increasing hubbub, people turning for their cars, and with a shock Matt realised the crowd was on the verge of panic.

"What are our options?" Claude's voice cut through the clamour and silenced it instantly. Thirty years in the top boardrooms in the country had left him with easy authority and money always talks. Before the hubbub could start again, Jill jumped into the gap.

"Evacuate the valley or make preparations to stand and fight."

"If we stand and fight what are our chances?" Claude asked.

"Low to nil. We have water supplies, but even if we stand and defend one house we couldn't extinguish a firestorm."

"We could put out the flames," Lindi protested.

"But the smoke and oxygen depletion would still kill you, mum." Her son's tone of voice indicated that he thought she, and most other grownups, were stupid.

"How likely is a firestorm?" Claude projected his voice easily, cutting off the teenager's next comment and preventing an imminent maternal explosion derailing the conversation.

"Jake thought it was a dead cert," Colin replied.

"Which leaves evacuation." Claude nodded thoughtfully. "Road?"

"The road out is blocked," Ben supplied.

"With the south ridge on fire, the trail bikes can't get out," Nick added.

"Which leaves climbing the cliffs or flying," Claude said. Looking round he shook his head slowly. "I don't think we will all be able to climb the cliffs."

"I'll stay behind if it means the others can get out." The quavering voice belonged to old Mrs Daniels, clutching her cat carrier to her chest. A few of the others, older or infirm, nodded agreement.

"The fire front moves sixty miles an hour, easily. I've seen it. We wouldn't be able to climb out before it caught us." Jim's comment was confirmed by Matt's nod.

"Matt, you said the crop sprayer could only take two?" Claude asked.

"Two at a time, but we'd have no time for a second run."

"Can we get outside help?"

"Jill's trying." Rose answered that one. "The Emergency Services are swamped, there are three larger towns being evacuated first. The coastguard don't have the manpower, since their air support's working with the main evacuation."

"The Air Force can get here but the troop carriers that can land here aren't particularly fast. Three hours to arrival." Jim's comment offered a ray of hope, quickly quashed. "If the fire gets into the valley, we'll have about twenty minutes before it gets here and if the airfield gets torched, they won't be able to pick us up."

"Which leaves the Shackleton as the only escape option we can prepare," Claude said. "Then we should work on the Shackleton, get it ready to fly, and if the emergency services get here before the fire then we go with them. Anyone who wants to stay should leave now to make their own preparations."

He looked round, but there were no dissenters. The Stilsons were already heading for their car. Claude waited a moment for any others to leave, then shrugged when none did.

"Fine. Nick, can you get to your house, take the trail bike and do a house-to-house? Make sure that anyone left is aware of the situation and then get back here. Hurry." Nick nodded, kissed his wife and climbed into his car.

"Jill?" Claude started, then saw she was already walking away.

"Radio duty. I'll try to get someone in to evacuate us more quickly."

"Good. Don't tell them about the Shackleton. We don't want to get bumped down the rescue list if they think we've got a way out." Jill smiled and nodded her understanding as Claude turned back to the crowd. "Matt, on to the Shackleton. What do we need to do?"

"Fuel her, make her load lighter, and figure out how to get everyone in. Rose, can you grab some volunteers and get her refuelling?" Matt had seen this coming and planned his response. Rose nodded, looking round and quickly gathered a few volunteers who followed her into the hangar.

"We'll need the runway checked," Jim added. "She's a lot wider than the crop sprayer, so we need all the obstructions cleared for a distance to either side."

"Fine. Lindi, can you manage the kids to do that, if Jim shows you what to do?" Lindi's surprised nod as Claude singled her out was quickly replaced by determination to do her part. The older children were quickly rounded up and led off.

"Anyone who isn't doing anything else, we need a firebreak set up by the road. Go down to the road through the valley where it borders the airfield and start clearing the brush and debris. Roger, you'd better go with them. Bill, you know how to build firebreaks, please show everyone." Claude's orders were quickly followed. As the crowd split off to their respective tasks, Claude turned back to Matt.

"They're all yours. I'll get them doing whatever you need, as long as it's reasonable."

"Do you expect this to work?" Matt asked.

"No." Claude's response was uncompromising but honest. "I expect the make-work will keep them from panicking long enough for us to get evacuated. But having a contingency is never a bad thing. "

"Jim and I will need to plan this anyway." If Claude's lack of faith shook him, Matt showed no sign. Instead he looked across to where Jim was walking back. Behind him the children and a few of the older residents had formed a line about an arm span apart and were sweeping down the left hand side of the runway in a reasonably disciplined fashion.

"Air Force discipline?" Matt raised an eyebrow.

"I told them I'd drafted them." Jim smiled slightly.

"Come on. If we're going to fly her, you need to know what you're flying." Matt's comment was met with a silent nod. Jim knew the Shackleton well, but not all the changes or fixes that Matt had made to her over the years. As they walked up towards her, he was struck once again by the sheer size of the aircraft. She was slightly smaller than the C-130's he normally flew, but on an airstrip built for light aircraft she seemed immense.

"Pilots manuals're in the cockpit. Come on." Matt climbed up the ladder into the aircraft, and Jim followed, turning right towards the front automatically. Carefully he climbed past the crew positions towards the cockpit, stepping up to get over the housings for the wing spars that ran through the cabin. He nodded at Jill, sitting by the radio, and slid neatly into the co-pilot's seat. Matt had already taken the captain's and was flipping through a pile of papers before he turned and simply handed the entire stack to Jim.

"Have a read. They'll tell you what you want to know."

"K."

"Might want to stay here for it. It's quiet. Remember she's live so don't touch anything."

"Understood." All Jim really wanted was time in the cockpit to get to work reading. "Anything I should know that won't be in here?" Matt frowned slightly, and looked round the cockpit. His lips were moving as he silently ran through all the work he had done and he began to shake his head before he stopped abruptly.

"Few of the gauges are a bit erratic. I haven't tested them all. Once she's flying, don't try and retract the undercarriage," he warned, and Jim frowned.

"Broken hydraulics?" There was a sudden silence from the other pilot's seat and

Jim looked across as a horrible suspicion dawned. "Don't tell me you welded it down?"

"I had to get the corrosion off somehow." Matt's defensive protest was almost indignant. "And I thought she'd spend the rest of her life standing on it."

"You welded it. You welded the undercarriage." Jim struggled to keep his composure as laughter, or possibly hysteria, threatened. "Do anything else to it I should know?"

"Added a few support struts. Extra strength, since she spends all her time on it." Matt's explanation did it for Jim who simply collapsed, virtually howling with laughter. The disgruntled pilot stood up and brushed himself off. "Fine I'll leave you with the flight manual." Rapidly he turned and left, awkwardly clambering over the raised housings for the wing spars that separated the crew positions. Jim shook his head and turned back to the panel in front of him.

After the wide view available from the cockpit of the crop sprayer, the Shackleton's field of view seemed oddly restricted. The yoke control instead of the stick demanded a different grip and approach to handling. No GPS screen was present, but then route finding would usually be the navigator's job. For this flight they would have to rely on visuals, but then they would not be flying high because she was not pressurised. The four main engine gauges lined up neatly down the center panel for either pilot's convenient view, instead of the yellow water tank gauge he had become used to. He reminded himself she would only be taking off on four of the possible six engines, trying to remember to allow for the loss of thrust. She could still get into the air, if she had enough space to build speed and a pair of capable pilots. Jim paused, settling his hands on the controls and closing his eyes. Almost unconsciously he shifted in the seat, inhaling the aircraft's familiar scent of oil, metal and leather. It had been years, but it felt briefly as though he had never been away. Awkward, ugly, and his very first military aircraft as pilot. Some things you didn't forget.

From behind him in the radio station he heard a quiet calm voice, and his eyes opened. Slowly, not wanting to disturb her, he looked round. Jill was sitting by the radio operator's post, headset in place, sending out a transmission.

"Once again, this is Radio Shackleton from Brooke's Vale. We are cut off. The cliffs to the north and east are impassible, and the fire front has surrounded the valley on the south and west sides. We have forty people gathered at Brooke's Vale airstrip who need evacuation." Her voice was as calm as if she were discussing the weather. "I repeat, forty people require immediate air evacuation. The fire is on two sides and all routes out are blocked. Please contact the Emergency Services if you can help." Jim swallowed. The unnatural calmness of her tone and careful enunciation of each word for transmission was almost eerie. She repeated her message one more time, giving GPS co-ordinates for the airfield, and then signed out. For a moment she sat stationary, hands clasped in front of her, eyes closed, and then she raised her head and pulled the headset off. Jim coughed politely, and stuck his head round the pilot's seat.

"I can always hope." Jill smiled faintly as she explained, and Jim nodded. "Better get back to the scanner and phones, just in case." She pulled herself out of the seat, and carefully raised a leg to try and climb over the three-foot high ridge across the cabin. Jim jumped out of

275

the seat and went to help. Even with past experience and the advantage of height, the spars across the cabin were sometimes awkward for him to get over and Jill was having problems. As he helped her to the ladder she smiled gratefully, nodded at him and then climbed down to get back to work. For a moment he was reminded of the doctor from the day before, and her stoic comment about drawing straws. That type of composure under stress was something he envied, and now drew on his own military discipline to emulate. Turning he climbed out briskly and walked across to Matt.

"I'm happy enough with it," he said by way of greeting.

"Then we need to know where to put people. Not a lot of room in there." The two of them looked along the length of the aircraft.

"The crew cabin at the back. Block the door if we have to." Jim was focusing on the problem of trying to fit thirty-three people into the small cabin. The crew seats up front would not hold many.

"Not worried about the weight aft?" Matt raised an eyebrow.

"Not really. People are light compared to what she usually carried. I'm more concerned about unrestrained passengers in the front. Last thing we need is people getting thrown into the controls."

"No parachutes," Matt commented, and Jim shrugged.

"Half the time we didn't wear them anyway." He was concentrating too hard on the aircraft, working out in his head where to fit people, to notice the sharp glance Matt threw him.

"Done many hours?" The question was entirely too casual.

"More than my share." Jim paused as he realised what he had said and sneaked a guilty glance at Matt. The older pilot was inspecting the bomb bay, a slight superior smirk on his face.

"Could we put anything in the bomb bay or nose position?" Matt asked thoughtfully, and Jim decided to go with the flow.

"No. What if we have to make a belly landing or crash?" His flat tone allowed no room for argument. "We just have to cram everyone in the cabin."

"Agreed."

"The runway's too short for her full run up and she's missing her jets. We're going to need her as light as possible to take off."

"A lot of my spares and tools are in there. They aren't secured," Matt replied, and looked at Jim.

"Then they have to come out. This is going to be a rough ride."

"And apparently we have to make room for Tigger, Shady, Duke and Tiny." Matt's voice conveyed his opinion.

"What?" Jim's voice was deadly quiet and Matt gestured to a small group of cages by the cars.

"They won't go without their pets." Matt did not say how lucky it was that only the four were present. It seemed most of the pet owners and those with livestock had left earlier.

"If there's room, fine. But we're not leaving people behind to make room for animals. And they go in cages. No free roaming." Jim's comment left no space for compromise and Matt obviously agreed.

"Claude?" Matt raised his voice slightly, and the director turned. "We need to get the animals stowed in the cabin if they're coming."

"We'll need one of you to show us where they go," Claude replied, his voice carrying.

"I'll be right across. We need to empty the fuselage anyway." Matt's answer was loud enough to be heard across most of the airfield and with a nod, Claude began to assemble another group. As the people split off to their adopted tasks, Matt caught Jim's arm.

"Once she's up, she'll fly. It's the getting up and coming down that worries me," he admitted quietly and Jim grinned.

"I know. But are you going to share that with the bunch of non-pilots out there?" He threw a nervous glance at his watch. "If the Chinooks don't make it, she's our only route out."

"This isn't going to work," Matt protested, despite knowing in his heart that it might. "She can't be certified to fly."

"You know damn well that doesn't mean she can't fly." Jim's voice was deadly serious and he stressed each word in his next question. "Matt, can this aircraft fly?"

"I." Matt paused and swallowed. His answer when it came was one word, virtually whispered, so low only Jim could catch it. The other pilot straightened up and nodded.

"Doesn't matter anyway. Let's get to work."

To take off on the shorter runway, with the passengers crammed inside, the aircraft needed to be as light as possible. The lovingly restored lifeboat was detached and discarded. Inside, anything remotely unneeded was ripped out and dumped. And in the background, watched over by a couple of the kids, the fuel pump chugged and churned as the giant aircraft was fuelled for one last run.

Behind the Shackleton, the smaller shape of the crop duster began to move. There were few in the crowd who did not feel the instant pang of fear, that the pilot would turn onto the runway and leave them to the flames. Instead he swung right, into the hangar. He taxiied her into the middle of the empty space and turned off the engine. Jim was across quickly, helping Matt out, and placing chocks against the wheels.

"Just getting her out of the way," Matt said. Jim nodded, saying nothing about the fact that C-SPRY 10 would stand a much better chance in the middle of the hangar than outside.

If it were not for the risks of smoke inhalation and suffocation, he would have suggested they all stay with her.

Everything finally in place, Matt walked out to the front of the hangar. He had one last task. With the help of a few willing volunteers, he pulled the hangar doors shut and secured them. If he paused for a moment before he turned to the Shackleton, no one commented.

"Any sign of your mates?" he asked rhetorically, and Jim looked at his watch, shrugging helplessly.

"Even if they left when they got the message, they'll be at least another hour."

"Well in that case better make sure we've got everything ready for them when they turn up." Matt rubbed his hands together, looking round as he inventoried everything to be taken. "We'll need to be out of here quickly. You all ready?"

"Shit," Jim spat suddenly. "I need to get back to the house." He took a step away from Matt and ran directly into Rose.

"Why?"

"I left something important there," he replied desperately.

"Is it alive?" she asked and he blinked. "Is it alive? Yes or no."

"No."

"Then it can wait. There's no time." The urgency in her voice was unmistakeable, and she pointed towards the south ridge. The smoke was rising in dense clouds from behind the rise.

As the two argued, Roger paused and took a few steps away from the aircraft. His jaw dropped quietly open. Nick turned to say something and then stopped as he saw Roger's expression and followed his gaze.

Irregular puffs of smoke had been rising from behind the south west ridge. With the fire on the other side, and the wind carrying most of the smoke away unseen, the scale of the disaster had remained mercifully hidden.

Now, along the tree line at the top of the cliff the trees were moving and thrashing as if in a gale. A few flickers of red and gold visible even over the distance showed that the fire had topped the ridge. Then the trees turned to flame as they watched, and the isolated patches of fire joined, turning the horizon into an inferno.

Temporarily it halted, as if thwarted by the sparse vegetation and rocky outcrops at the top of the hillside. Then, almost tentatively the first tendrils of orange began to reach down the hillside and into the valley. Matt took one look at what everyone else was now staring at and raised his voice.

"Everyone, clear of the plane. I'll get in the cockpit. Jim, we're starting the engines, get the fire extinguishers ready." Hurriedly his orders were obeyed, although once clear of the plane, most of the crowd went back to staring at the fire that was making its way down the hillside.

"The Stilsons are up there," Rose whispered.

"You can't help them." Jim's cold response drew a few stares. "Head up there now, you'll die as well." Rose nodded without saying anything.

Before them, part of the fire on the ridge seemed to separate, rolling and tumbling down the cliffside and into the valley. One of the ancient pines, dried and weakened in the long summer, had burned through. The sound of its crashing descent down the cliff was audible across the valley, only to be drowned out.

The first of the Shackleton's Griffon engines initially announced itself with a politely asthmatic cough as it wheezed in the smoky air.

As the long propellers began to turn, they stuttered slightly and then speeded up, appearing to reverse before blurring into reassuring invisibility as the engine's coughs settled into a low, formidable, growl.

The watching crowd's smiles turned to frowns, and almost unconsciously they began to back away as the second engine started. The noise that had spooked the Taverner's horses from the far side of the valley was almost painful up close, and they slowly realised that there were still two more engines to start.

"Is it that loud inside?" Claude yelled, and Rose shook her head.

"It's muffled by –" The rest of her reply was lost as the third set of propellers began to turn. She whipped out a notepad and scribbled a quick note on it, holding it up for everyone to see. In response to her quick request, which simply read "Ready to go?" she got enthusiastic nods, although most now had their hands over their ears.

The fourth and final set of propellers began to turn. There was something vaguely hypnotic about their movement as they came up to speed, almost like a kaleidoscope as the blades turned smoothly in opposite directions.

Jim was watching nervously, aware that the aircraft had been remarkably well behaved until now, and hoping the engines did not live up to their usual reputation.

He was in luck. The four engines settled to emit the steady low growl of a Shackleton ready to take off. From the cockpit Matt's thumb's up sign was barely visible, but barely was enough. Jim herded the crowd far enough back that he could be heard and raised his voice.

"Last chance to back out. If you want to stay, now's the time." There were a few incredulous glances at the south west cliff, now ablaze. Small smoke plumes showed where hot ash and falling debris had settled, starting smaller fires.

"Fine. Form an orderly queue and keep clear of the propellers. Rose, can you direct them?" Rose nodded, and Jim turned and ran back, climbing into the aircraft to get settled in the cockpit.

Carefully the first of the passengers stepped up the ladder and into the Shackleton. Rose tried not to laugh, despite the gravity of the situation. Once he got back, Nick had been in and out of the aircraft, carrying boxes, spares and anything else that Matt said could be removed. Now it was time to get in as a passenger he was suddenly, obviously, nervous. Torn between the desire to cover his ears from the noise and the need to cling onto the ladder while buffeted by the wind from the propellors, Nick climbed up almost gingerly. At the top the big man ducked his head automatically as he climbed in, and then turned and offered a hand to the next one on the ladder, his twelve-year-old son whose enthusiasm could not have made a more obvious contrast.

As the refugees climbed in Rose checked them off against her list. She had taken the names of everyone she knew was here to make sure no one was left behind by mistake. Then she realised one was missing. With the engines running she had no chance of being heard if she shouted, and she climbed up the ladder quickly, shouting into the doorway for Jim. The passengers inside heard her and relayed the message, as the pilot scrambled back towards the entrance. Even right by him she had to shout to be heard.

"Jim, can you get Jill? She's still inside with the radio."

As Rose slid back down the ladder, Jim followed her and ran back to the office. Rose was reluctant to leave the bottom of the ladder, trying to fight down the image that someone would climb out when her back was turned and be left behind. As the other two ran back, Rose saw Jill was clutching the mobile phones. As she climbed in, the older woman shook her head.

"Sorry, nothing on an official evacuation. The Chinooks are on their way, but otherwise they say they can send someone else in an hour. They've declared it a firestorm officially now but the forces are at full stretch, and there are bigger towns than ours under threat.."

"That'll be too late," Jim said flatly as he followed her up.

"Yes. They estimate the fire will be here in ten minutes or less," Jill agreed grimly as Rose bundled in behind them. As Jim shut and secured the door ready for take-off, it hit Rose what they were trying, and she caught his arm. With the others so close she could not say anything, but he understood anyway. He gave her a brief half smile, and finished what he was doing. Mercifully the engine noise deadened somewhat as the door closed.

"Right, people, we don't have much time. Get settled in crash positions. We're going over rough ground so expect jolts. If you can secure yourselves against anything please do." Jim's voice echoed inside the fuselage, and he tried to remember he was not in a military aircraft now. If he gave orders, his audience would revolt. "There are a few seats and crew positions available here and here. Put anyone who can't get thrown around in those, and the rest of you get as secure as you can."

He turned and headed up to the front where Matt was already sitting. Matt had naturally taken the captain's seat so Jim slid in next to him.

"You know these things used to have a crew of ten, right?"

"Yep." Matt, utterly unflappable once he was in a cockpit, continued to run through his checks. His eyes strangely distant, Jim knew that the vision before his co-pilot was his precious plane in flight, and quickly began his own checks, afraid that in his enthusiasm Matt would miss something. Even as Jim did, Matt shrugged.

"We're wasting fuel. Are you ready?" he said sharply. He did not wait for an answer before he increased power slightly and the engine note from the Rolls Royce Griffons perceptibly deepened.

Eight propellers thirteen feet long bit into the air as the Shackleton began to roll forward under the power of all four engines. Despite their best attempts, the village had found nothing able to tow the large aircraft, and it was left to Matt to position her using the aircraft's own power. Almost painfully slowly she turned on to the runway, straightening as Matt lined her up for take off.

Both pilots cast a glance at the windsock, but it was tossing nearly randomly in the gusts from the fire. All it told them for certain was that they were taking off directly into the wind.

And then with a jolt and a rumble she accelerated. Matt, unused to flying with passengers or a co-pilot, had seen no reason to announce his intent, and simply brought the throttles to full. If they were going to take off they needed to gain as much speed as quickly as possible.

The Shackleton's engine note took on the characteristic growl. Slowly at first, as if she was gathering herself and then with a rush as the engines responded, the huge aeroplane surged forwards on its take off run.

In the back there was a faint gasp, unheard over the engines. Despite their words no one had really believed she would fly, and yet now as the Shackleton thundered along the tarmac it suddenly seemed possible.

Jim watched the instruments carefully, trying not to mutter the litany running through his mind: the list of all the things that can go wrong on a normal take-off, far less an aged defunct aircraft like this. Tyre blow out, engine failure, metal fatigue, control surface failing... then he looked up and flinched despite himself. The Shackleton's take off speed was much higher than the crop duster's, and it was easy to forget what that translated to in distance. Matt was staring impassively ahead, hand tight on the controls, and the end of the runway was approaching with frightening speed.

Abruptly they ran out of runway. The huge plane smashed through the narrow wooden fence bounding the field at the end and kept going. The bone-jarring rattle in the cabin became worse as the wheels churned and cut into the dry surface, but at almost a hundred miles an hour, the sheer momentum of the twenty ton aircraft kept it going, and accelerating.

There was nothing of grace or style in this, her final take off run. Instead the engines' guttural growl, and the bone jarring shuddering from the rough ground all combined to give the impression of sheer brute strength as the Shackleton fought for the sky one last time.

The juddering slowly lessened and in the back Rose cautiously looked up. Ahead of them she could see only fire.

"Keep her low. Build speed." Matt's voice was surprisingly calm, and Jim nodded in the co-pilot's seat. Then he ruined the effect by adding:

"Oh god, don't let us lose an engine now." She could see why. Ahead of them, at the edge of the field, the trees were wavering and bending as if in a storm. Beyond them smoke and flames reached out of the forest, licking upwards towards the sky. They were almost on them.

"Now!" Matt's cry was almost simultaneous with Jim's and as both pilots reacted, the plane tilted into a climb. As the settled growl of the engines took on a deeper note, the passengers found themselves beginning to slide towards the rear of the plane as the angle of the climb increased. All engines struggling in the poisoned air, the Shackleton climbed into a sky full of sparks.

"Five hundred feet." Matt reported, concentrating on the climb. "We need more altitude."

Risking a look, what Rose saw outside looked like a scene from hell. The pines were wrapped in flames, towering candles in the sea of fire below them. The air churned whitely with ash, and above them a bloated red sun was faintly visible behind the thick grey-brown cloud that rolled and swirled over the fire. The hill at the end of the valley was ablaze, and if they could not climb quickly enough the Shackleton would surely crash into the burning forest she could see ahead of them. The flames sweeping across the ground raced under the aeroplane.

With an impact that reverberated through the cabin the aircraft yawed, tilted and lifted. The unsecured passengers were thrown helplessly across the cabin, ending in a tangle of limbs against the side of the fuselage.

"Thermals." Matt exclaimed, and the tone of his voice was strangely victorious. The aircraft tried to tilt again, but this time the pilots were ready and responded, bringing her level and into a climb that the passengers could feel. The fire that swept towards the town and endangered them now brought with it the hot air that lifted the huge aircraft.

"Hold her steady." Matt had to raise his voice over the twin roars of the engines and the inferno below them. Jim nodded grimly, trying to keep the Shackleton climbing smoothly as the thermals drove her upwards. The aircraft was vibrating under the strain, and he hoped silently that she would not shake herself apart from the stress.

Then suddenly sky was ahead of them, black and filled with ash and smoke, but not flames. They had cleared the ridge, and the ground below them fell away. All they could see beneath them, to the limits of their vision in the clouded air, was fire.

"Where now?" Matt asked, almost quietly. Getting to Lakeside in this was impossible. Too many other aircraft and risk of collision, even if the Shackleton could make it that distance in these conditions. The little airfield he had in mind as a backup would be gone, evacuated and maybe even burning.

"Aim for the far side?" Jim responded, still battling to keep the Shackleton climbing as turbulence buffeted the aircraft. The engines stuttered uncertainly, choking on ash.

"We'd never make it. Crash land on trees in this?" Matt shook his head frustrated. "She'd break apart."

"The sea! Turn north." Jim's sudden decision was announced as an order.

"But the fire – "

"The road's blocked, not the sky. We'll fly round on the thermals and splash down. It's only twenty miles direct." Jim risked a quick looked at Matt, who was already nodding. The course would take them back over the valley, but that could not be helped. The ash and smoke were so thick that visibility was virtually nothing. Beside them, the huge propellers that turned only feet away were no more than dark shadows through the ash and grime rapidly obscuring the cockpit window. He turned north on instruments, watching the compass, and then froze. Quickly Jim tapped the instrument panel in case it was the display that was stuck. No such luck.

"Shit. We've lost the altimeter."

"Tube's clogged. Just try and get her as high as you can." Matt was trying to remember the terrain between here and the coast. He was sure there was another cliff but if they were not high enough, in these conditions, they would not see it until impact.

Beneath them, the valley was a solid mass of flames sending smoke and ash spiralling upwards. The pilots focused on controlling the aircraft as it bucked in the unpredictable thermals from the firestorm forming in the valley. The Stilson's house could hardly be seen through the churning flames. Of the owners, valiantly determined to not be driven out, there was no sign. Huddled in the back, listening to the growl of the engines and the roar of the inferno beneath them, the refugees closed their eyes and prayed.

"Can you get anyone on the radio?" Jim asked, as Matt fumbled with it.

"Either no signal, or it broke on the take-off," Matt growled, trying to check it.

"Can any of you get a signal?" he yelled back, hoping the passengers would hear him. "Radio's out."

A few of the passengers had already fumbled out mobiles and were dialling frantically, but there was no signal. All the emergency service lines were tied up with other calls and it was impossible to get through. Then from the back:

"Gran? Gran! Listen, it's me, we're in the Shackleton, we're heading straight north to splashdown. Gran if you know any – Shit." Rose's despairing wail was punctuated by the steady beep as her phone lost the connection. She went to throw it against the cabin wall, but Jill grabbed her arm.

"Keep dialling! You're the only one with a signal." Rose stared at her wide-eyed and then nodded, frantically punching buttons in an attempt to restore their lifeline.

"Did anyone grab the radio from the crop sprayer?" Jim asked. Matt shook his head.

"Fine. How are we doing on fuel?"

"'Bout ten minutes flight left at this rate," Matt replied "I'd guess we're only five from the coast."

"You guess?" The outraged roar from Roger in the back interrupted them. The door between the back of the fuselage and the main cabin had opened and now he stood up, grasping a strut for support and making his way towards the cockpit. "Don't you even know where we are? Why the fuck did I even get on here? We could have stayed back there and –"

"Shut the hell up, Roger." Jill's eyes were blazing. "No one forced you to come."

"When I take orders from a bitch like you –" Roger staggered as the plane shook. Matt had finally had enough and turned on him.

"Shut up or get out. You weigh two hundred and fifty pounds. That's an extra thirty seconds of flight for the rest of us. Wannabe a hero? Door's that way."

"Matt!" Jim's sudden cry brought the captain's attention back to the front. The passengers found themselves tumbling to the back of the cabin.

The massive wave of heat from the end of the valley had flung her nose up, and the Shackleton teetered, angle of attack suddenly too high.

"Jesus Christ, she's gonna stall."

"I can't get the nose down," Jim yelled, working the controls urgently.

"Turn her!" Matt yelled back. Caught in turbulence that threatened to push her so far over that she would simply fall out of the sky, the aircraft's controls hardly worked.

"Dammit," he muttered, trying to force the plane to bank, to change the high angle into a banking turn that the Shackleton could come

297

out of, anything to break the grip of the thermal forcing the aircraft's nose ever upwards. Either they had to ride it out and pass through it, or turn away. There was no chance of recovering from a stall in these conditions.

The aircraft groaned and shuddered under the strain, as Matt fought to change the brutal climb into something they could ride out. For a moment he was afraid the Shackleton would stall anyway, slipping sideways into the flames. Then sluggishly, the aircraft began to respond, and as the wingtip raised an instant later, he knew they had succeeded. A moment later and they were past it, the fire behind them.

Carefully he brought her back to the level, checking the compass. They were still headed north, and then a small glimpse through the smoke ahead renewed his resolve.

"Matt. The port engines." Jim's quiet statement brought Matt back to their predicament. A quick glance showed him the gauges veering wildly.

"Which one?"

"Both."

"Can anyone see the port engines?" Matt hollered back. There was a general scramble as the passengers tried to see either wing, not sure which one 'port' was.

"They're on fire!" The blunt response from one of the kids left the pilots sharing a horrified glance. Jim reacted first, reaching for the fire control system he knew so well, flipping the switches to trigger the extinguishers in the engines. They moved limply under his hand.

"Where's the fire control?" He stared at the fire warning lights, still dead, and reached for his belt strap, ready to head back to investigate the problem.

"At the barn. I hadn't finished repairing it yet." Matt was cutting the fuel flow to the engines even as he spoke.

"Power dive to put them out?" Jim suggested, turning back to the controls, and Matt shook his head.

"She'd never survive the strain."

"Jettison fuel?" Matt shook his head again.

"Flying time. Can we pump it to the good engines? Damn it we're so close!" Jim looked where Matt was pointing and gasped. Through a spot in the clouded glass ahead of them he could see a glimpse of water, the deep blue of the ocean he knew so well.

"Everybody, brace for landing," Jim shouted back, and then there was no more time for talk as both pilots focused on bringing the aircraft down in one piece.

The Shackleton's engines could be heard before the aeroplane came into view. Jake pulled his crew back into shelter, uncertain of what he would see or where they would come down. When the call came in his had been the nearest crew, and he had immediately been assigned the rescue mission. The coastguard boats, not usually recruited to deal with forest fires, had seized the chance to help and their rescue vessels were standing by out of the expected crash area. All he could do was wait, listening to the engines approach, and hope that they would make it down in one piece.

The big aircraft screamed into view. It soared over the cliff edge, missing it by what seemed like inches. The undercarriage was down, but barbed wire and wood wrapped the struts and had destroyed the wheels, and the underside of the aircraft was pitted and blackened. Charred, and trailing smoke from one wing where the propellers turned aimlessly before the crippled engines, the aircraft's nose lifted as the pilots tried to make sure she would land flat.

"Holy – she can't land like that." The fire marshal's appalled comment drew nods as the aircraft almost fell out of the sky towards the bay. The rescue team watched in horror as she slammed into the shallow water, kicking up a wave that enveloped the beach.

Almost without slowing, she ploughed onwards, towards the sea. The tip of one wing, stressed too far, simply sheared off by the damaged outer engine. The propellers disintegrated, sharp metal shrapnel peppering the sand and sending firemen diving for cover.

Finally, the noise stopped, and the rescue crew looked out cautiously. The Shackleton was lodged sideways across the sandbar towards the bay entrance. Her nose and fuselage were mostly clear of the water, but her undamaged wing was fully submerged, probably lodged against the sand at the bottom of the shallow water. The stub of the other stuck pitifully up into the air and streaks of fuel down the side of the battered aircraft spoke of a new danger, that of fire and explosion. Jake glanced across the bay, where the spreading pattern on the water indicated the risk was not confined to the aircraft itself.

"Get a boat out there," Jake snapped, but the order was unnecessary. The ridged plastic lifeboat was already being pushed into the water by its eager crew, while the coastguard vessels moved in from the sea. It took only moments for them to reach the wreck.

One of the coast guards jumped out, guiding the shallow boat up the sand bar until it beached. As the crew piled out, they scrambled up the slick sides of the fuselage, past the door and up to the shattered wing. A propeller turned slowly, its single remaining blade churning the air. The gears and engines that drove it were destroyed, and it swung back and forth purely from the momentum of the crash. Smoke curled up from the remains of the engine beneath it. Finding the wing too steep to climb, one of the firemen leant against it, reaching up as far as he could and spraying foam from a portable extinguisher.

Assisting his efforts, a white spray arced from behind the aircraft, raining down on the raised wing. A red-hulled fireboat had come as close as it could in the shallow water and was carefully coating the engines with retardant foam.

"Call the boat off." The urgent message came in from team B on the fuselage, and Jake complied. The spray died away.

"What's the issue?"

"It's like an ice rink up here. The foam's making it worse and she's rocking as the spray hits. It's too unstable." The spray had done some good, Jake noted however, and smoke no longer curled from the upper engine.

As a second extinguisher was passed to the fire fighter on the wing, the crew jumped and carefully moved back, slipping and sliding on the smooth surface. In the midst of them the heavy door in the fuselage swung downwards, into the aircraft, leaving a black hole visible from the shore. A moment later and two hands stuck out. The crew swiftly kneeled by the doorway and gripped the raised arms, pulling the first of the evacuees out and helping him to balance. Carefully the boy was helped clear and the next began to exit.

"How many are there?" The voice crackled across the radio.

"About forty." Jake signalled back. The second evacuee had obviously heard them because she stopped, saying something to the fire fighter who was helping her, and pulled out a sheaf of papers.

"We have a passenger list." The signal came back, and then a query "Identify Rose Hamilton?"

"Part of the C-SPRY 10 team," Jake signalled, and then answered the unspoken question. "Good in a crisis."

"Request Rose remains here to identify casualties."

"Confirmed." Jake frowned slightly then realised the problem. Soaked with spray and wearing thick gloves the fire fighters would have problems managing Rose's list, which was doubtless home made. As he watched the first boat was quickly loaded, and six casualties brought back to shore, all women and children.

"Jake! Good to see a familiar face." Lindi's greeting was pure relief.

"Nice to see you. I'm managing the crew here. Could you go with the EMT's to get checked out?" Jake's tone was professional and reassuring. Lindi was not the most stable of the people he knew from the Vale, but this time she nodded confidently and began rounding the kids up to go with the medical staff. He had only one vital question to ask. "Is everyone in there?"

"No. The Stilsons stayed." Her face changed to a mask of utter horror. Jake could not swear in front of her, although he wanted to. Instead he turned to the radio operator.

"Request the Air Force attempts a pick up from the Stilsons' house. It's number 39, on the south west side of Brooke's Vale." He nodded at Lindi. "Believe me, we'll do everything we can." She smiled back, slightly shakily, and then the medical team hustled her off with the kids. Jake turned his attention back to the rescue, trying to ignore the nagging thought in his mind that the Stilsons were dead.

"The Chinooks will be there in five minutes," one of the team supplied, and he nodded.

The ridged boat had already arrived back by the sandbar. By the fuselage door, the problem of getting survivors off the slippery aircraft had been solved by hooking the top of an unfolding ladder into the door entrance, trailing it down what would usually be the aircraft's top and securing it on the sandbank. A small crowd of evacuees was already waiting their turn to be ferried back to shore.

Further along the sandbank, the fireboat

had pulled in close and was standing by. Another fire crew was wading through the shallow water, onto the sandbar and across to the wreck.

"Team C in position. Checking for survivors."

"Team B preparing to enter the fuselage."

On the aircraft's body the first of the fire fighters to enter the fuselage braced himself with a hand either side of the doorframe and lowered himself carefully into the Shackleton feet first.

"Need lights in here." Quickly sets of portable lights were passed in. With the aircraft on its side and half the windows blocked the inside of the Shackleton would be very dark. Light would not just help them get the casualties out; it would reduce the stress on the survivors and the chance they would panic.

"Can't get to the cockpit. Nose wheel pushed up into the fuselage." Jake tried to ignore the sudden cold chill he felt as he heard the signal. "Getting mobile casualties out."

"Put the coastguard helicopter on standby for medevac." Jake told the operator, looking down the beach at the cleared car park.

The red painted helicopter's blades had begun to turn, stirring a faint breeze even this far away. With them all on the same main frequency, all the teams could hear each other. It was a fair bet that there would be at least one casualty requiring medical evacuation. The ridged boat had beached again and a second set of stunned survivors was being led across to the medical facilities.

With a lot of flesh wounds and broken bones expected, the medical crew had set up a makeshift field station on the promenade below the cliff. Jake had already heard complaints about the sand getting into everything, but ignored it. With medical facilities onsite to deal with emergency treatment for the walking wounded and the severely injured being airlifted straight to the nearest hospital outside the danger zone, the evacuees had the best chance he could give them.

"Chief, it's the Chinooks." The younger crewman turned away from the radio and looked back. "They say they can't land at Brooke's Vale."

It took a moment to sink in. The large troop carrying helicopters were designed to land on or hover over most surfaces. If they could not put down then the fire must have filled most of the valley.

"Any chance of winching anyone up?" Jake asked, already knowing the answer. The radio operator gave him a sympathetic glance. He knew where the crew chief lived.

"Sorry. The whole valley's on fire and the turbulence gave them problems flying over it. No chance to lower a winch. They didn't see any survivors."

Jake nodded and turned his attention back to the shattered aircraft. He could grieve later, but for now his attention had to be getting as many evacuees out of the plane alive as he could.

"Can you request the helicopters come up here to assist with moving casualties out of the fire zone?" There was a pause as he waited for their response, and then the radio operator nodded.

"Sir, acknowledged, and they're heading up here."

"Good. Get someone to clear the car park down the beach for them to land." Jake drew a breath. If they could move the walking wounded to the hospital by helicopter it prevented the need for a convoy to evacuate them through the fire danger zone, blocking roads that the emergency services needed clear.

A shout carried across the water, and one of the firemen from Team C round the aircraft's nose gestured frantically.

"Survivor in the nosecone." The plexiglass nose that usually housed the aircraft's cannons was vibrating violently. Jake had seen the same in cars, a trapped casualty kicking at the windscreen to try to get out. One of the crew reached up and knocked on the glass, letting the casualty know they were there.

"Request power snips." The calm voice came over the radio, and Jake relaxed slightly. The crew chief on Team C was a reliable experienced fire fighter. If either of the pilots could be saved, he was one of the best to do it.

"Suspected heart attack. We need medevac." The signal from team B brought his attention back to the main body of the aircraft. Down the beach the coastguard helicopter was gearing up for take-off.

"Coastguard, co-ordinate with Team B on the fuselage," Jake ordered. If everyone inside was walking and conscious it would have been a miracle. After the last few days he no longer believed in them, and was just praying most had survived. Even as the helicopter lifted away, Jake asked for more details. He did not have to wait long for an answer.

"Mr Randell, age 82. Generally good health and apparently no mental impairments."

"Apparently?" the helicopter pilot queried. He had heard the dubious tone in the fire fighter's voice.

"Between wheezes he keeps laughing and saying at least he's not going to burn. Happiest heart attack victim I have ever seen in my life." The fire fighter's voice conveyed his utter disbelief.

"He's got a point." By this time the helicopter was hovering over the aircraft, its winch lowering carefully. The fire fighters clustered round the door carefully passed the end of a stretcher up through the doorframe and out onto the top of the aircraft. The winch man knelt by the stretcher and carefully secured it. After a few moments of painstaking work, the fire crew stood back, the helicopter winch powered up and the stretchered casualty was drawn rapidly upwards. Loaded efficiently into the hovering machine, the helicopter swung about heading for the nearest hospital. It would be back shortly to repeat the operation.

Meanwhile, more of the mobile casualties were being helped out and queued on the sand.

"Team D to control. Permission to move the boat inside the sandbar and assist in the evac." Jake blinked. He had forgotten the smaller Coastguard rescue boat had a shallow draft.

"Granted." With an extra boat, removing the survivors would be a much faster affair than the four or six that the ridged marine boat could take at a time. The crew of the coastguard vessel wasted no time in hauling their boat quickly over the sandbar and into the bay by main force. Immediately they began to load the survivors.

Jake looked round for the head of the medical team, and got a quick acknowledging nod.

"Can you get an onsite team ready? The risk of fire should be under control."

"They're on standby." The medical team leader was way ahead of him, and several of the medical staff who had heard them were picking up equipment ready.

"Good. Send them back with the next boat." As the man nodded Jake turned back to the radio operator. "Let the crews know the EMTs are coming onto the sandbar."

Around the nose the fire crew stepped back. Several of them had headed to the boat and returned with axes, crowbars and rescue equipment, and the plexi-glass nose had been swiftly removed. Jake blinked, trying to remind himself he should be co-ordinating all the teams, but at the same time his personal worries were getting in the way. With the fire crew gathered round the nose he could not see what was going on. Silently he tried to tell himself that anyone getting out alive was a bonus, that either Matt or Jim surviving would be a blessing, and yet he knew with guilty certainty he was praying for his brother to live.

The sound of an engine distracted him and he looked up. The small white helicopter was not one that he recognised, and as they flew out over the wreck he scowled. The radio operator was already on the public frequencies telling them to desist, before Jake saw the three letters on the side of the helicopter and immediately knew what the answer would be. Freedom of the press.

"Chief, they say they –" the radio operator began, and Jake cut him off.

"Tell them that they are interfering with the rescue, and their downdraught could unbalance the wreck. If it does, we'll charge them with murder. It's not reckless endangerment if they've been told they're going to kill someone and do it anyway." After working on the fire front he had had enough of the press. He had no issue with responsible journalists, but then responsible journalists were not the ones standing in front of a fire front to get the perfect shot, asking casualties how it felt to have lost everything, and phoning in asking for rescue from areas that had been evacuated before they had sneaked in. Right now, with his family and friends' lives at stake he was not playing games.

The EMT crew were unloading by the aircraft as another set of casualties stood by to get in. With medical staff actually at the crash site, the survivors had a much better chance. Once the mobile casualties were out it would be time to deal with the more severely injured. That was when, as Jake well knew, the official death toll would start to rise. Two of the paramedics were rushed to the nose, but Jake could not seem to focus on the group as his sight blurred.

"Get out of my way!" The frustrated exclamation from the radio brought him back to the fuselage and the airspace above it. The press helicopter had found its perfect space for a shot into the aircraft, right where the coastguard helicopter needed to be to winch up casualties. Reluctantly, it seemed, the press helicopter pulled away. As they manoeuvred, their downdraught kicked up a spray that dowsed the wrecked aircraft, survivors and fire fighters in spilled fuel. Jake saw red.

"Call the police. Now." He instructed the radio operator. "The helicopter – " he squinted through the binoculars and read off the call sign " – is interfering with a rescue and just created a fire hazard."

"Sir, the police are very overstretched. But the coastguard are right here." The radio operator pointed out. Jake could have kissed the man.

"Then please notify the coastguard that the fire service want to press charges."

"Believe me, so do the coastguard. We're rather busy right now." Came back the pithy response from the helicopter pilot. He was already lowering his winch again and another stretcher was waiting on top of the fuselage. Jake's attention was drawn away from the press helicopter.

On the beach the boat was coming back

with another set of casualties, although from the voices carrying across the water one of them was not too happy about being rescued.

" – not the Captain, you're a civvie so shurrup and be rescued." The voice was unmistakeable and on shore a couple of firemen looked round, giving their chief odd looks. The boat's crew were carefully wearing their best poker faces as they beached it and started helping the walking wounded out.

"Rose is still helping out there." The plaintive complaint was almost a whine.

"Rose doesn't have broken bones, a concussion, and a face full of broken glass."

"But she's my plane." There was a definite note of desperation in the voice.

"Matt, if you're going to be a hero, why couldn't you be the strong silent type?" The blanketed figure climbing out had drawn the attention of several of the crew by now, and Jake decided to get it over with. Looking at his second, who was more than aware of the situation and grinning broadly, he headed down the beach.

"So, are you the ones I should be doing for littering?" He gestured at the wrecked plane. His voice had carried further than he thought and Matt and Jim both turned suddenly, staring at the fireman walking towards them. It was a bad joke, but it got a vague grin from Matt at least. As Jim looked up, Jake's shock showed. His brother's face was a solid mask of blood. He froze, looking him over, about to call for a medic when his brother laughed shakily.

"Scalp wound, and a lot of flying glass. It's worse than it looks." Jim paused, obviously parsing out the sentence in his head. "I mean it's not as worse as it looks."

Jake noticed the slightly unfocused look on his brother's face and jumped back just in time, as Jim was suddenly and violently sick. As the medical team rushed across Jake shook his head while Jim tried to apologise.

"Normal reaction to this type of thing. Go and get yourselves seen to. That's an order!"

The lead medic took Jim's shoulders and carefully steered him towards the medical tent. Behind them Matt followed, his face tinged grey and tremors running through him. He had his arms held up in front of him, crossed but not touching, and flinched whenever someone went near them. Jake swallowed hard. How bad had conditions in the Vale been to force them to take a gamble this desperate? How bad must it have become that the townsfolk would come with them?

The second boat was returning, this time only partly full. He recognised Rose among them, pale but composed.

"Is that it?" Jake asked. As the medical team began to empty the casualties, the boat captain nodded.

"No other mobile casualties. We'll leave Team D on standby, but the rest will require airlifts. Ms Hamilton, remaining passengers?" Carefully Rose pulled out a plastic bag where she had folded the list to keep it dry on the way back and took a breath to read it off. Gently Jake took it out of her hands.

"I'll make sure this gets to the right people. You get to medical."

"I – " she protested, looking at the list and not his face, obviously not recognising him.

"Rose, you've just been in a plane crash. Medics now."

"Jake?" She had not come out of the crash unscathed, he realised. The colours beginning to show down her arm were not dirt but a huge bruise, matched by the one emerging on the side of her face. He looked at the paramedic, who carefully put a blanket round her to ward off shock and began to walk her towards the medical bay.

"Jim's up there," Jake added as they left, and suddenly her footsteps picked up. He chuckled slightly, handing her notes to one of the medics who headed up the beach at a flat out run, and then his smile vanished as he saw the fuselage. The press helicopter was taking advantage of the coastguard's absence to swing back for another pass. This one would run along the length of the sandbank, but the downdraught would be dangerous. He turned for the radio, but even as he did he heard the engine note change, growing louder. The press helicopter swung sideways and lifted away abruptly.

"What's got into them?" he wondered aloud.

"Probably them." The radio operator sounded rather pleased, and pointed to the sea. As the sound of engines grew louder the two Chinook helicopters swung into view round the coastal cliff, high but descending fast. Carefully they avoided the wreck, swinging over the beach before one of them settled on the car park the coastguard helicopter had used as a base. The other one took up patrol further out to sea.

"They did say that in two minutes they were going to be in this airspace, and if the press 'copter was in their way then obstructing the military could result in being accidentally shot down, and then the coastguard could arrest any survivors." The radio operator was grinning widely. Jake frowned. He did not know if Chinooks were armed. Apparently nor did the press.

"They aren't going to come off well in the press over that."

"Err, chief. I think it's that helicopter that's not going to come off well." The radio operator gestured up the cliffs. Just visible at the top of the slope a reporter's van was set up, and another journalist was doing his own piece to camera. The letters on the side did not match the ones on the helicopter, and a coastguard official seemed to be talking earnestly to the anchorman. Jake felt a sudden wide grin cross his face, and then went back to work.

"Confirm with the St. Mary's Hospital that the helicopters have arrived, and keep them updated." He looked round for the lead medic, only to see the man's back retreating across the beach as he headed for the Chinook. Inside the medical bay, the first set of casualties was being prepared for their airlift. The severity of their injuries and the need to make sure they were secure meant it would take time, but it would still be faster and safer than moving them by road.

"Any update on the fire front?" he asked anxiously.

"They've held it fifteen miles south." The answer was good news, he supposed, but it felt so very hollow. He turned back to the fuselage, watching as the coastguard helicopter returned for its next casualty. The white helicopter was trying to manoeuvre to get a good shot, but the Chinook pilot was blocking it carefully, preventing them from interfering in the rescue.

"What's the white helicopter? Why aren't they helping?" Jim had walked down from the medical bay behind Jake and was now frowning at the drama being played out before them. Without having to worry about the press helicopter, the coastguard could move faster, and the stretcher was already being fastened to the winch.

"Press. Damn vultures. Obstruct the rescue teams so people get killed and make the news covering the deaths they cause." Jake's tone was pure acid, and Jim threw him a startled glance. Whatever had happened over the past few days it seemed his brother had had it harder than they had. "Too bad your base couldn't send an Apache."

"Doesn't carry enough people. I can't believe you got this all set up so quickly. It's only been ten minutes since Rose called."

"Blame Radio Shackleton." Jake gave his brother a disgruntled stare and then chuckled at the look on his face. "One of their listeners let the station know what you were up to a couple of days ago, and they decided to make it a regular feature. When DJ Raucous Ricky heard you were going to try and fly out, he mobilised his audience. Nearly jammed our phone lines."

"Oh." Jim sounded absolutely floored.

"Yeah, you can say that. We had to let him know you're down. If he's going to get his listeners to phone in sightings he could have told them what the damn plane looked like. I think you've been every large aircraft for two hundred miles. Excuse me." Jake turned back to the fire crew. The stretcher had reached the helicopter and the helicopter crew were pulling it inside to secure the casualty ready for the flight to the hospital.

Jim stepped back to let Jake work, and Rose stepped up behind him, taking Jim's hand with her good arm. They took a few steps and settled down on a rock out of the way. Matt shuffled down to join them, looking a little less grey, both arms wrapped in splints and bandages across his torso.

The team on the fuselage were not waiting for the helicopter to return. Once again a stretcher was drawn out again, but this time something was wrong. The crew stabilised it, turning it sideways with care and there was no urgent rush of EMTs to the casualty. As it moved, they saw that the sheet had been pulled up over the face.

"Who?" Jim asked bluntly, his face a mask.

"Mrs Daniels," Jake said, quietly as he turned to arrange for the body to be brought back by boat. No sense wasting a helicopter trip on the deceased. Jim looked at Rose, the question unspoken.

"She was too frail to survive the crash. Her neck snapped on impact." Rose saw no kindness in fudging the answer. Anything she could have said, that at least the old woman died quickly, that the flight had given her a chance, that she was with her family, would ring very hollow. Jim already knew all the words. Instead she touched his arm and gestured silently across the sand. Bill Jones and his wife were standing by the edge of the surf, watching. As the stretcher was removed, placed on a boat to return to shore, Bill looked away and saw them. He squared his shoulders and walked across, stopping short as if trying to find what to say.

"I am so sorry for your loss." It was all that Jim could think of to say, but seemed so pitifully inadequate. Beside him, Matt's utterly stricken expression said more than words.

"Not your fault," Bill said, and his voice cracked. He coughed to clear it. "Might as well say it was mine. If we'd got out earlier, when we heard your first warning –"

"The fire," his wife said quietly, giving her husband time to compose himself. "They'll say it was the crash, but it was the fire that was responsible, and the bastards that started it. If it weren't for the fire none of this would have happened. I make that twice today you've saved our lives."

"Reckon mum would think me a mite ungrateful if I blamed you." Bill's chuckle came out as halfway between a laugh and a sob. He stepped forward, looked for a part of Matt that was uninjured and settled for clapping him gingerly on the shoulder. He nodded once, unable to speak, and then turned back to the beach where the boat was pulling in. Slumping, taking his wife's hand for support, he walked back to say his goodbyes.

The sound of engines turned heads across the beach. The rescue workers had cleared back and now the Chinook's two long rotors were beginning to turn. As the blades gathered speed, blurring into invisibility, they kicked up dust across the beach. Several of the rescue workers turned away, shielding their eyes. Then, carefully and perfectly level, trying not to jar the casualties inside, the helicopter lifted. It cleared the level of the cliff and almost delicately turned in the hospital's direction before it began to move, accelerating smoothly as it set off on its mercy mission.

Above them on the cliff-top, a small crowd had gathered. Cameras were beginning to flash, and Jake quietly thanked his luck that the bay was isolated and behind an evacuation line. The two roads down had been cordoned off the moment the rescue operation had begun, and unless anyone could free-climb or fly, they were unlikely to be interrupted.

"Sir, it's Cordon One. They say they have some of the relatives there." Jake sighed. He was used to press tricks to get access to rescue sites.

"Any names?"

"Yes. Mrs Hamilton. She says she got the phone call." Jake blinked. It was quite likely that it really was Rose's Gran up there, but it did not change what he had to do. It simply meant that he would never hear the end of it.

"Tell her they aren't allowed down. The casualties are being moved to St Mary's, so relatives can meet them there. The fire front is too close."

Jake had other things to worry about. Out by the Shackleton, there were five more stretchers in position, ready for the coastguard helicopter to pick up. One of the coastguards caught his arm to get his attention, breaking him out of his thoughts.

"St Mary's is at capacity, sir."

"Call round anywhere that may have spaces." Jake gritted his teeth looking round at the stretchered figures waiting for an airlift. His mood was not improved as the boat began its return trip, two bagged figures in it. Removing the corpses was necessary for rescuers morale and sanitary reasons, but he had to force himself to detach, to not think about the fact these were friends he had lost. The lead medical officer walked across from the bay, his face grim.

"We have three here that need medical attention urgently."

"There are five more on the sandbar." Jake nodded agreement. "We're trying to find space for them now."

"Excuse me. St. Johns say they can take them." The coastguard broke into the conversation, holding a phone. Jake bit his lip. St Johns was twenty-five miles further down the coast than St Mary's. Evacuating one at a time it would be hours before the last casualty could be sent there, and time was always critical for patients in that condition. A sudden idea struck him and he looked out past the wreck.

"Think that press helicopter is still a problem?" Jake asked rhetorically. As he looked round he could not see it and the skies seemed clear. He turned back to the crewman with the phone. "Ask St Johns if they have space for a Chinook to land. A car park or field will do."

Turning to the radio operator he continued. "Check with the Chinook. Can they take critical casualties up to St Johns?" He turned to the medical staff lead, who nodded.

"I'll get teams ready to go with them."

The agreement from the Chinook crew was decidedly enthusiastic, but then so far their only duty had been to run off press helicopters. Now they had a role to play in the rescue itself.

Rather than move the stretchered casualties to shore, both boats were brought back, and the three casualties loaded in. Medical teams and supplies were sent with them. Once everyone was unloaded onto the sandbar, the difficult part of the operation came into play.

The Chinook carefully descended over the sea at one end of the sandbar. Turned to minimise its impact on the crash site, Jake could still see the dust and sand it kicked up as it hovered, ramp open and just touching the bar. As it held position the casualties were loaded inside. The attending medics ducked their heads and ran in, their supplies being handed up behind them. Then the fire crew stood clear, sheltering behind the wrecked Shackleton. Slowly the Chinook's ramp closed, and then with the same exaggerated care as its predecessor the helicopter lifted clear. Only when it had reached an altitude where its downdraught could hardly be felt did it turn and begin its journey to the hospital.

Jake let out a breath, pausing to gather his thoughts. Only twelve casualties left, and they were all on the beach. His part of the rescue was nearly over, and then he could hand over to the cleanup operation and investigation.

"Check with the Chinook at St. Mary's," he said, reflecting that he really should have remembered their call signs. "Can they take the remaining casualties to St John's?"

"They say no problem. They'll be back here in about twenty minutes." Jake nodded, relieved. It was one thing to know why they preferred to keep service personnel off cases involving friends and family, quite another to have experienced it. "I'll let the evacuees know. Any families we had to separate?"

"Only three, the Jones, Georgesons and the Barnehursts are still here." The crewman said, referring to Rose's increasingly battered list. Jake ran down it at a glance and then closed his eyes as the breath went out of him. Not all families were linked by blood, and he threw a glance across the beach to where the three were still sitting. He could see Matt's mouth move, and knew what he was asking even though he could not see it. Slowly he begin to make his way across, hating the news he had to give, but knowing that there was no one better to tell the pilot.

"Jill?" Matt asked quietly, almost bewildered. He had been looking round, quite lost, and it was obvious who he was looking for. Jim looked across at Rose as she stiffened, and raised an eyebrow in a silent question. Rose broke his gaze, staring at her hands and wondering what to say. As Matt looked round again, she decided that the truth would be the best. She had been standing on the side of the aircraft when they had found the office manager and keeping her composure as they pulled Jill clear for the airlift had been one of the hardest things Rose had ever done.

"Unconscious. Suspected skull fracture and a lot of broken bones." Rose's expression was grim and did not hold out much hope. "It could have been worse. She was going back from the radio position when the plane dived. She'd been trying to get a signal out for help."

Matt shuddered. The radio operator's

position no longer existed. The reinforced strut of the undercarriage had torn through it and the other crew positions when the impact drove the wheel up into the fuselage.

"My fault," he muttered to himself. Rose stared at him, reaching out her good arm and then seeing the bandages and thinking better of it.

"Matt, it's a plane crash, these things happen," she protested.

"My fault. Stupid mistake…" Matt shook his head, and Jim stepped forward and gripped the top of his shoulder, forcing Matt to look up.

"You couldn't have known. It was never meant to fly again. And we'd all be dead back there if we'd stayed." Matt looked at him and then pulled free, sitting down with his head in his hands. Rose lifted a questioning eyebrow at Jim, who jerked his head. In silent agreement they stepped away.

"What do you mean? It is his fault?" she hissed, appalled.

"The undercarriage is supposed to have weak points, so they snap or crumple in a crash instead of driving up into the fuselage. Matt welded supporting struts over them to strengthen the undercarriage while he worked.

We never had time to take them off." Jim explained miserably and Rose pressed a hand to her mouth.

"That's – oh god. Poor Matt." Awkwardly, with the blanket round his shoulders, Jim put his arm round her as she leaned on him and hid her face. He could feel her shaking as the reaction of the last few hours finally set in.

"Come on. It's pretty much all over now. Get to the hospital, get checked out, go – " he paused, realising he could not say home, and amended it quickly " – to the Moorlands."

"Yeah, which reminds me. Why were you so desperate to get back to the house before the plane lifted off?" Rose shifted uncomfortably, trying to ease the ache in her bruised arm. When the plane had crashed she had been slammed sideways into the internal doorframe. Grabbing it had saved her from worse injuries, but the ache in her shoulder indicated it had taken a price. Too many people she knew were dead or injured and she wanted a distraction, anything to stop thinking about what had just happened.

"Yeah well." Jim shuffled a bit. "I wanted to get something. I had a promise to keep for Jill."

"Oh?" Rose's curiosity was piqued. Jim sighed and stood up, looking round the beach. Bits and pieces of the aircraft were scattered across it, torn free like shrapnel as the Shackleton had struck the water and disintegrated, and it took him a few moments of searching to find what he was looking for. Carefully he limped back and came to a halt in front of her.

"Sorry, I think my legs stiffened up. Now Rose, let it never be said I'm not a man of my word. You're good in a crisis, you can fix my car better than I can, and I promised Jill that if I ever got you up in a plane with me I'd do this." He looked at the sand and, carefully, painfully, lowered himself down on to one knee. Taking a breath he held up a little rubber washer from the Shackleton.

"Will you marry me?"

Some Months Later

Two months later and as the season changed, the Vale still bore the scars. Most of the valley was covered in charred remains and the silent shells of burned out houses still stood as a monument to the lost.

Here and there were signs of life returning, birdsong and green shoots springing up. Even a few of the burned trees appeared to be recovering. Across the valley, sparsely located, a few new homes had been built where the old had been torn down. It would take time but the Vale was recovering.

The evacuees had been allowed to return a week after the fires were out to gather their possessions and survey the damage. The firestorm had taken everything, leaving only charred remains and fine white ash on the valley floor. The Stilson's house was a skeleton. Mercifully the fire crews had already been in and recovered the remains of the family. Once the road was blocked, no one made it out of Brooke's Vale alive who wasn't on that plane. It was a simple fact, and one that had the plan to prosecute Jim and Matt for flying an uncertified aircraft quietly shelved.

At the airfield, they had discovered the burned out shells of the cars they had abandoned. Twisted beyond all recognition, several burst open where their petrol tanks had exploded, all they were good for was scrap and the insurance companies had quickly agreed. Ironically Matt's own fuel store had not exploded as feared, but there was no fuel left in it. Even the fuel vapour appeared to have burned away.

The smell of smoke that had escaped when Matt had opened the hangar, and the fine white powder of ash on all the surfaces had finally settled the question of whether the survivors would have been better off staying in there. Even the crop sprayer had not come through unscathed. The intense heat had warped the surfaces, wing plates lifting and loosening. The ash had made its way deep into the workings and the entire aircraft would need to be disassembled and rebuilt before they would know if it could fly again.

It had been a final blow for Matt. He had turned on his heel and walked away. The next day he announced he was selling the airstrip. Despite the people from Brooke's Vale he had saved, he could not clear his memory of the people in the car he had failed. He was moving his remaining aircraft, the Robin and C-SPRY, to rented hangar space at Lakeside, and had bought himself a small cottage by the airport. The occupants were only too glad to get away from the sound of planes, while Matt wanted to be closer to them. Jill went with him, saying she was too old to rebuild a house from scratch. The Lakeside was right by one of the better hospitals for her ongoing treatment, and she hoped to be flying again soon. Walking could take longer.

Jake had moved back soon afterwards, and he and Jim had spent hours picking through the pieces of the house for the insurance claim.

As Jake said, the Vale had had its once in a century fire, so should be safe to live in for a few more years. The presence of the fire marshal had brought confidence back to the valley and more of the survivors had returned. As people reasoned, he had been correct about the fire, so if he moved back he was probably correct about it being safe. He planned to rejoin the fire service full time, once he was done directing the rebuilding.

The buzz when the burned out airfield and the plot next door were both sold to a mystery buyer only intensified when the builders moved in. Over the next weeks the field was restored, a new hangar built and large engineering works took place late into the night. Matt refused to comment on a private business transaction, but the mystery was quickly solved when the first planes moved in and the new owners came to look round.

"You've really done this place up." Rose looked around the airfield in appreciation.

"A good use of the press money, right?" Jim grinned, understandably proud of himself. In the months since the fire all the survivors had been contacted repeatedly by the press. The reporters called the story "human interest" while Jill preferred "nosey parkers". While the survivors were of passing interest, the pilots had been in great demand and Rose's Gran had quickly fixed them up with a publicist who had helped them make the most of it. The press money had been extremely useful while they waited for the insurance companies to sort out the payments for repair and rebuild. In between the press conferences, discussing with his superiors about his future career plans (and possible use in Air Force recruitment) Jim had had the building contractors in, levelled the damaged buildings, replanted the trees, and rebuilt the entire set up. Now the little airfield was one of the few areas of the valley to be almost fully recovered. By the next summer the traces of the fire would be gone.

"So, why did you wait two months to tell me you bought it? And what makes you so sure I'd live here anyway?" Rose asked archly.

"Well let's see." He leant on the car's bonnet and started counting off on his fingers. "One. I've built our new house well away from the airstrip. Two. Can you think of anywhere else I could have got a few hundred acres at this price? When it regrows it'll be lovely. Three. It will more than pay for itself. With the number of airfields that were levelled and the prices that Lakeside charges there are a lot of people after cheap hangar space. I've got customers already. You still don't look impressed." Rose shook her head at him, gesturing for him to continue. He sighed theatrically. "How about four: I got the plans for your dream home from your Gran. The ones you've been working on since you were twelve? I built the house to that design. It's not quite finished, but we need your input before – "

He was abruptly cut off as Rose squealed and hugged him then let go, suddenly deadly serious.

"Does it have the workshop?" He nodded, grinning, as she hugged him again.

"However, there is one condition attached," he said seriously.

"What's that?" The arms tightened uncomfortably and she sounded suspicious.

"Come on, it's quicker to show you." He undid her arms from round his neck, and took her hand, walking up towards the brand new gleaming hangars. The extended strip of tarmac bays for the planes was neatly marked out, and had not been down long enough to gain the marks of oil and dirt from an established airstrip. It was also partly occupied, and Rose looked puzzled. There was a brand new micro-lite, sitting next to two planes she didn't recognise.

"I see Claude got himself a new toy plane, but what are the others?"

"The Cessna is Claude's other new toy. He said he'd prefer to make his own way out next time."

"And that?" She paused by the gleaming white biplane and Jim chuckled.

"Terry Sacorski's Antonov. His airstrip's unusable and Lakeside costs an arm and leg. Besides, Matt asked him to take over his crop spraying since Matt's training as an aerial firefighter."

"Matt? But he's sixty!" Rose exclaimed in surprise.

"You think that would stop him?" Jim's wry comment made her stop for a moment. Then she laughed and shook her head, looping her arm back through his and resuming the slow walk to the hangar.

"Nice to hear he's got plans. By the way, Gran tells me there's a divorce in the offing," she commented casually, and gave him her best innocent look as Jim frowned at her. "Emily –

that is, Mrs Roger – was not too happy about her husband's attempt to leave her here to die. And then there was the matter of the beach hut. Did you hear what was in it?"

"No idea." Jim was not usually one for gossip, but then nor was Rose, and the question had puzzled him for a while.

"His mistress. Apparently they'd arranged to meet there before the fire really caught." Rose stopped as her fiancé burst out laughing.

"That's just – hold on, did she make it out OK?"

"Yes, she was miles from the fire. No, Roger's rush was because he couldn't get her on the phone and wanted to tell her not to contact him. When the network came back up, all her queued messages went to the voicemail and he wasn't the one that picked them up. They're now in the hands of his wife's lawyer."

"Ouch."

"Between that and the whole "leaving her and the kids to die" angle, it looks like the former Mrs Roger is going to make out rather well."

"Do they need anyone to testify about his attempt to run off?"

"Too late. Matt's filed a statement. He said it was the most pleasure he's ever gained from completing a legal form. With what I had to say about his attitude to women, and his attempt to damage the Robin and assault an evacuee, he's also down as having anger issues."

"So, a happy ending then." For some reason, Jim could not get the smile off his face. Finally at their goal, the larger of the two gleaming metal hangars he paused and fidgeted.

"Now Rose, once I'd bought the airfield, and done the house, and invested a bit for a rainy day, I had a bit left over. And then the insurance payment came in."

"Really?" One sardonic eyebrow lifted.

"And Matt showed me the figure for scrap value from his insurance. And well, it left enough to get some decent engineers in..." He trailed off. Rose's jaw had dropped open in disbelief.

"Jim, tell me you didn't." He looked at her with a hangdog expression, reached up a hand to the main hangar door and pulled it open with a flourish.

It stood in stark contrast to the gleaming metal of the hangar, scaffold cradling the cracked fuselage and keeping the weight off the ruined undercarriage. Grass and soot had marred the gunmetal grey finish and white lines of salt showed where it had been sitting in the sea for days before it was recovered. The wings stuck out, one complete, the other ending abruptly in twisted, sheered, metal.

"I never took you for a sentimental sort, Jim Roberts."

"I'm not. There's a guy down the coast selling an intact airframe for parts. With the bits from both, we'll have her flying again in no time. And there's a certain heavy metal station that wants to do a special broadcast from the cabin." He sighed. "And I'm completely transparent, aren't I?"

"Totally, but it's very sweet. Come on, I want to see the house." As they walked back to the car, Jim smiled to himself and took her hand. Behind them the airport windsock flapped and billowed in the breeze as the wind changed, clearing the smoke and bringing the fresh smell of the sea to the valley.

--- The End ---

Afterword & Acknowledgements

Even an adventure story like Fire Season, which employs a fair degree of artistic licence, requires research and investigation. Readers who don't baulk at a cropsprayer pilot having a Shackleton in his hangar will rightly complain if the aircraft doors open in the wrong direction.

Therefore, my thanks to the people who made this possible: to Fred for sparking a lifelong love of aviation, and to the people (you know who you are) who put up with my endless queries about the Dromader.

Also particular thanks to Peter Mills and Peter Vallance at the Gatwick Aviation Museum for the information they provided on the Shackleton, and their patience with my numerous questions. In particular, thank you for the chance to have a look inside Avro Shackleton WR982, one of the two remaining runnable Shackleton Mk3's, at the museum Open Day.

Any errors that remain are, of course, my own.

Coming Soon

~

Days at Brooke's Vale

~

A collection of short stories set in and around the Vale before the fire season that changed it so much.